Carole Mortimer

WIFE BY CONTRACT, MISTRESS BY DEMAND

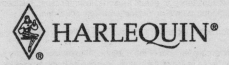

HARLEQUIN®

TORONTO • NEW YORK • LONDON
AMSTERDAM • PARIS • SYDNEY • HAMBURG
STOCKHOLM • ATHENS • TOKYO • MILAN • MADRID
PRAGUE • WARSAW • BUDAPEST • AUCKLAND

ISBN-13: 978-0-373-12633-0
ISBN-10:   0-373-12633-6

WIFE BY CONTRACT, MISTRESS BY DEMAND

First North American Publication 2007.

Copyright © 2007 by Carole Mortimer.

This edition published by arrangement with Harlequin Books S.A.

® and TM are trademarks of the publisher. Trademarks indicated with ® are registered in the United States Patent and Trademark Office, the Canadian Trade Marks Office and in other countries.

www.eHarlequin.com

Printed in U.S.A.

HARLEQUIN®
Presents~

Outside, the weather is getting hotter, and here at
Harlequin Presents, we've got the books to warm
the temperature inside, too!

Don't miss the final story in Sharon Kendrick's
fabulous THE DESERT PRINCES trilogy—
The Desert King's Virgin Bride—where Sheikh Malik
seduces an innocent Englishwoman. And what
happens when a divorced couple discover their
desire for each other hasn't faded? Read
The Pregnancy Affair by Anne Mather to find out!

Our gorgeous billionaires will get your hearts racing....
Emma Darcy brings you a sizzling slice of Sydney life
with *The Billionaire's Scandalous Marriage,* when
Damien Wynter is determined that Charlotte be
his bride—*and* the mother of his child! In
Lindsay Armstrong's *The Australian's Housekeeper
Bride,* a wealthy businessman needs a wife—and he
chooses his housekeeper! In Carole Mortimer's
Wife by Contract, Mistress by Demand, brooding
billionaire Rufus uses a marriage of convenience to
bed Gabriella.

For all of you who love our Greek tycoons, you won't
be disappointed this month! In *Aristides' Convenient
Wife* by Jacqueline Baird, Leon Aristides thinks
Helen an experienced woman—until their wedding
night. Chantelle Shaw's *The Greek Boss's Bride* tells
the story of a P.A. who has a dark secret and is in
love with her handsome boss. And for those who
love some Italian passion, Susan Stephens's *In the
Venetian's Bed* brings you Luca Barbaro, a sexy and
ruthless Venetian, whom Nell just can't resist.

Dinner ^{at} *8*

Don't be late!

He's suave and sophisticated.

He's undeniably charming.

And, above all, he treats her like a lady.

But beneath the tux, there's a primal passionate
lover, who's determined to make her his!

Wined, dined and swept away by a
British billionaire!

All about the author...
Carole Mortimer

CAROLE MORTIMER is one of Harlequin's most popular and prolific authors. Since her first novel published in 1979, this British writer has shown no signs of slowing her pace. In fact, she has published more than 150 books to date!

Carole was born in a village in England; she claims it was so small that "if you blinked as you drove through it you could miss seeing it completely!" She adds that her parents still live in the house where she was born, and her two brothers live very close by.

Carole's early ambition to become a nurse came to an abrupt end after only one year of training due to a weakness in her back, suffered after a fall. Instead she went on to work in the computer department of a well-known stationery company.

During her time there, Carole made her first attempt at writing a novel for Harlequin. "The manuscript was far too short and the plotline not up to standard, so I naturally received a rejection slip," she says. "Not taking rejection well, I went off in a sulk for two years before deciding to have another go." Her second manuscript was accepted, beginning a long and fruitful career. She says she has "enjoyed every moment of it!"

Carole lives "in a most beautiful part of Britain" with her husband and children.

"I really do enjoy my writing, and have every intention of continuing to do so for another twenty years!"

PROLOGUE

'WHAT the hell do you think you're doing?'

Gabriella raised long, sooty lashes to reveal eyes of so deep a blue they appeared violet, to look across the terrace at Rufus, the man she had fallen in love with a year ago when her mother had married his father, the man her eighteen-year-old heart desperately hoped would fall in love with her, too!

She had heard his hire-car arrive on the gravelled drive at the front of the Gresham family villa in Majorca. She forced down her nervousness and remained stretched out on her lounger soaking up the sun, rather than running to greet him as she wanted to do. Rufus, she had quickly learnt, was not a man that you ran after, but instead waited for him to come to you—even if he was the love of your life and just looking at him made your knees tremble with longing!

He stood in the doorway that led out onto the terrace, having removed the jacket to his light business suit in the intense heat of the early afternoon. His overlong hair was the colour of molasses, glinting golden in the sun, and his eyes—

a piercing pale green, Gabriella knew—were hidden behind the black sunglasses he wore.

But his question, and that disapproving slant to his chiselled lips, were enough to tell her that he wasn't at all pleased at finding her sunbathing alone on the terrace, in a bikini comprised of small scraps of orange material.

Deliberately so. Rufus had a habit of either treating her as an irritating child, or of totally ignoring her altogether. But she so much wanted him to recognize her as a desirable woman.

'I'm working on my tan, Rufus, what does it look like I'm doing?' She smiled, at the same time stretching languorously, arching the slenderness of her back, the movement forcing forward the fullness of her breasts, her nipples visibly aroused in her nervousness through the bikini's orange fabric.

'I can see that, damn it,' he bit back scathingly. 'For goodness' sake put some clothes on, will you?' he snapped as he stepped outside onto the terrace.

'I'm topping up my tan, silly,' she said poutingly. 'And why should I bother putting clothes on when there's no one around to see me but you?' she added with tentative provocation.

It was one thing wanting Rufus to see her as a desirable woman, something else entirely actually maintaining this provocative pose!

The Gresham family villa, 'Bougainvillea', was perched alone on the side of the mountain overlooking the terraced village below, with a one-hundred-and-eighty-degree view of the Mediterranean.

Why bother, indeed? Rufus acknowledged impatiently, grateful for the black shield of his sunglasses that hid his emotions as his gaze swept slowly over Gabriella's lithely perfect body, already tanned to a golden brown and glistening invitingly from the oil she had smoothed over her torso, arms and those long, long legs.

It was a beautifully slender body, without blemish, that only the very young possessed, and that would be hard for any man to resist.

And Rufus had had plenty of practice at doing *exactly* that since Gabriella had burst into his life a year ago, making no effort to hide her infatuated interest in him.

An interest, at thirty years of age, he'd had no intention of satisfying!

Or, at least, he hadn't had any intention of satisfying until he'd walked out onto the terrace a few minutes ago and seen her lying there…

'Anyone could have walked out here and—'

'"Anyone" didn't, you did,' she reasoned cajolingly. 'Besides, the women on the village beach won't be wearing any more than this.' She frowned.

The village beach, Rufus knew from past experience, would be full of families at this time of day, most of the women wearing bikinis, some even topless, yes—but they weren't alone with the man they had been shamelessly infatuated with for the last year!

'Where are your parents?' he demanded harshly.

A little desperately, he acknowledged with inward self-impatience. At least the presence of his father and Gabriella's mother, his stepmother, would alleviate this situation. Even if he still found Heather's role as his stepmother almost as irritating as having this gloriously beautiful creature as his stepsister.

He was only here at all because he had stopped off to visit his father for a couple of days on his way back from a business trip to mainland Spain.

'James wanted to go into Palma some time today to buy my mother something wildly extravagant for their anniversary, but they should be back in a couple of hours.' Gabriella sat forward slightly, her violet-coloured eyes smokily inviting now as she looked up at him. 'They waited in for you this morning, but when you didn't arrive they checked with the airline and were told that your flight had been delayed for three hours. It's Margarita's afternoon off, too.' She shrugged bare, glistening shoulders. 'So I said I would stay here and wait for you.'

Damn, damn, damn. Not even the Gresham Majorcan cook and housekeeper was here to act as chaperone!

'Don't look so disapproving, Rufus.' Gabriella looked a little uncertain as she obviously sensed his displeasure. 'Or is it just that you're feeling a little hot and dusty from travelling?' she considered concernedly. 'Why don't you go for a swim?' she suggested with that naturally husky voice that alone could send a shiver of awareness down Rufus's spine.

Gabriella Maria Lucia Benito.

Daughter of Heather and the deceased Antonio Benito.

Apart from that deep violet of her eyes, Gabriella had inherited all of her colouring from her Italian father, her hair a glorious swathe of tumbling black curls that fell femininely down the long length of her spine, her skin naturally olive in complexion, but tanned a sleek mahogany from the weeks she had already spent at the villa.

But as far as Rufus was concerned, her mother, who had

been living in rented accommodation with her young daughter and had had to work as James's secretary in order to support them both, had only married his father because he was a millionaire many times over and the owner of the prestigious Gresham's, a London-based store that had a worldwide reputation for exclusivity.

Heather's daughter, the beautifully stunning, exotically sensual Gabriella, as far as Rufus was concerned, had just as calculatingly decided that he, James's only son and heir, would make an equally suitable husband for her!

There was only one problem with that line of thinking—Rufus had little intention of ever marrying again. He had tried that once, only to discover that Angela was solely interested in the Gresham money, too, walking out after only a year of marriage, and leaving their two-month-old daughter behind when she did.

Their divorce, six months later, had been messy and very public, resulting in Rufus giving Angela half his vast personal fortune in order to maintain custody of the baby daughter he knew Angela had no interest in anyway.

And into that maelstrom had walked Gabriella Maria Lucia Benito, when his widowed father, obviously having learnt nothing at all from Rufus's experience, had announced in the same breath that he intended both retiring as Chairman of Gresham's, in favour of Rufus, and marrying the attractive fifty-year-old widow who had been his secretary—his secretary, for heaven's sake; how clichéd was that?—for the last year, bringing with her a seventeen-year-old daughter from her previous marriage.

Tall, with a natural grace of movement, Gabriella, in her fitted tee shirts and tight, tight jeans, had taken one look at Rufus, it seemed, and thereafter done everything in her youthful power to tempt him into acknowledging her as a woman every time he visited his father at Gresham House in Surrey, her hungry violet gaze seeming to follow him everywhere.

But Rufus's own experience with Angela—even if he ever did contemplate getting married again, which was highly unlikely, to give his now two-year-old daughter a mother—meant that Gabriella Maria Lucia Benito, no matter how alluring, would be the very last girl he would choose. One grasping gold-digger in the family—her mother!—was quite enough, thank you.

But, he decided with another sweeping glance at Gabriella she was without doubt a beautiful girl.

'I think I might just take a dip in the pool,' he murmured throatily, starting to unbutton his shirt. 'The parents will be gone another couple of hours, you said…?'

'Yes,' Gabriella confirmed huskily, watching covertly as he stripped the shirt from his darkly tanned and muscled torso before unbuckling the belt on his trousers, unzipping them to drop them down onto the terrace exposing long and powerful legs.

The black fitted boxers he wore made more than adequate swimming trunks. But she blushed as she took in the dark hair on his chest, that moved down in a vee before thickening again, and her eyes widened as she saw the evidence of his arousal.

Rufus wanted her!

Gabriella swallowed hard, slightly breathless as her gaze

returned to the hard, uncompromising planes of his face, those pale green eyes still hidden behind the dark glasses.

Dropping down onto the side of her lounger, the touch of his thigh searing hers, Rufus drawled, 'Would you rub some oil on my back for me?'

Her hands shook slightly as she tipped some of the oil into her palms before moving to touch the broad width of his shoulders, loving the way his muscles tensed and flexed as she smoothed the oil into his skin, fingers softly kneading as she moved down the length of his spine.

Never, in her wildest fantasies about this man—and there had been a lot of those this last year!—had she ever thought he would allow her to be here like this with him, touching him, his hard strength making her tremble, a warmth between her thighs spreading as she felt the sexual tension between them grow.

'Now the front.' Rufus turned to lie back on the lounger, at last taking off those sunglasses to look up at Gabriella as she now sat beside him.

Gabriella rubbed the oil into his chest, her breath catching slightly in her throat as she felt herself captured by that totally assessing gaze as it moved over her.

'Lower,' he invited, seductively soft, one of his hands moving to rest on her thigh.

She could feel the warmth in her cheeks, her gaze avoiding his as she looked down at her tanned hands moving over his slightly paler skin, his stomach tautly muscled.

'Lower, Gabriella,' he urged throatily.

So much for showing Rufus how sophisticated she was, Gabriella thought nervously as her hands shook so much as she tipped more oil into them that she splashed some of the liquid onto his stomach and thighs.

'Yes, there,' he encouraged achingly.

Her touch was driving him insane, Rufus acknowledged. He breathed a short sigh of relief as her hands eventually moved down the long length of his legs. As it was, the featherlight touch of her fingers on his thighs and muscled calves did little to alleviate his ache, those caressing fingers on his legs increasing the need he had to make love to her.

But he shouldn't…wouldn't.

They had a couple of hours before the parents returned, Gabriella had said, and he intended touching her in the same way she had just touched him. Touching, but *not* taking.

'Now you,' he murmured gruffly as he moved to sit up and gently push Gabriella down on the lounger.

Rufus looked deeply into her eyes, taking his time as he rubbed the oil into his hands before moving them down to anoint her, Gabriella's groan of pleasure caused a similar response in his own body.

Yes, he was going to enjoy touching this sleekly provocative young woman. Every inch of her!

Gabriella couldn't look away from Rufus, totally enraptured by the sensations he was creating inside her as he caressed and massaged her with oil.

Just when she thought she couldn't bear it any more Rufus pulled away from her, raising his head to look down at her, eyes dark with satisfaction.

'Lower?' he prompted throatily.

She could barely breathe, let alone speak, the brush of her

lashes down against her cheek answer enough as Rufus tipped more oil on his hands to move down the slenderness of her waist.

Once again he held her gaze as he touched her, Gabriella's thighs moved sensuously against him as he increased the rhythm of his caress, feeling her arousal deepening and increasing as she hurtled towards a pleasure she had never known before, arching against him as that heat spun out of control and wave after wave of sensation ripped through the whole of her body, sobbing low in her throat, her hands moving up as her fingers became entangled in his dark blond hair, holding him against her as those waves became a crescendo of feelings that had her clinging to Rufus in unashamed abandon.

She had never experienced anything like this in her life before, none of her romantic daydreams about Rufus having prepared her for the reality, for her completely uncontrolled response to his caresses.

She had never felt as happy before as she did at this moment, knew that Rufus couldn't touch her in this way if he didn't love her, too.

She smiled dreamily as she imagined a future with Rufus. As his wife. How surprised her mother and James were going to be when they told them the news. They—

'Not bad, Gabriella,' Rufus derided softly as he looked down at her, his eyes no longer hot with arousal but coolly assessing. 'Very responsive, in fact,' he dismissed dryly as his gaze moved over her with clinical appreciation. 'But I think you had better go and make yourself decent before the parents get back,' he added mockingly. 'We wouldn't want to shock their sensibilities, now, would we?'

Gabriella blinked up at him frowningly, her eyes dark smudges of purple, not quite sure of him now. Rufus had just caressed her in a way no one else ever had, had taken her to a climax beyond her wildest dreams. Admittedly, they hadn't made love, but surely the intimacy they had just shared had to mean something to him—

'I think I'll go for that swim now.' He stood up, stretching languidly. 'And then I think I'd like something to eat,' he added dismissively.

He would like something to eat? They had just made love—well…Rufus had just touched her!—so how could he just calmly start talking about food as if—?

'What's the matter, Gabriella?' Rufus looked down at her with those coldly assessing eyes, his mouth twisted derisively. 'Not satisfied yet?' he mocked throatily. 'Well, give me a chance to have a swim and something to eat, and maybe I'll be in the mood for more of the same—'

'Why are you being like this?' Gabriella sounded pained, tears swimming in the deep purple of her eyes.

'Like what?' Rufus came back tersely, not falling for those tears; Angela had shed ones just like them every time she hadn't been able to get her own way during the total of eighteen months they had been together. Crocodile tears, totally deceptive, totally false.

Gabriella blinked dazedly. 'But we just—'

'No, Gabriella, you just,' he corrected hardly. 'You've been wanting me to touch you for the last year, and now I've done so…' he shrugged '…so what are you complaining about?'

She shook her head. 'I don't understand…'

'Gabriella, I've been stuck in an airport and an airplane for a total of seven hours,' he reminded impatiently, determined not to be swayed by the bewilderment in those deep purple eyes. 'I'm tired and I'm hungry,' he snapped. 'If you want any more from me then you're going to have to wait until I've satisfied at least one of my other appetites!'

She reached up to readjust her bikini top before answering him. 'But I thought—' She shook her head. 'I thought you and I—'

'Thought what?' Rufus's patience snapped completely. 'That you would seduce me—as you've been trying so hard to do this last year!' he added scathingly. 'And that I would then ask you to marry me, that I would behave like the lovesick fool my father has over your money-grasping mother? Well, think again, Gabriella,' he bit out coldly. 'I've already given all that I have to give where you're concerned!' His top lip curled back sneeringly. 'If you want a repeat performance, perhaps I'll be willing to oblige. But later, not now.'

Gabriella stared up at him tearfully.

She loved this man. Had thought his response meant he'd loved her in return. But his response, it seemed, had only been physical. A physical response he'd had complete control over as he'd taken her to climax, his comments since meaning to humiliate her—and succeeding.

Worse, he had called her mother money-grasping—her wonderful mother, who had known such misery when married to Gabriella's father, and deserved every moment of the happiness she had now found with James.

'Rufus, you can't seriously believe that my mother... She

loves your father very much!' she protested, wondering what that made her if Rufus could believe those things about her mother.

'Oh, give me a break!' he scorned hardly. 'It's easy to love someone when they're worth the millions my father is.'

'But she really loves him!' Gabriella defended heatedly.

'Of course she does,' he sneered. 'Enough to accept him giving her a hundred thousand pounds to pay off her debts before they were even married, anyway. A little excessive for a dress allowance, wouldn't you say?' he added scathingly.

'What?' Gabriella gasped, standing up. 'I don't know what you're talking about.'

'Oh, come on, Gabriella,' he sighed wearily. 'Just accept that I know about the money and the debts, and let's move on, shall we?'

She really didn't know what he was talking about, was sure there had to be some sort of mistake. Her mother would never— 'You're just bitter and twisted, Rufus, because everyone knows that Angela only married you for—' She broke off, realizing she had gone too far as she saw Rufus's face darken ominously. He seemed to loom over her now, his green eyes so pale they looked silver.

'Yes?' he prompted softly, dangerously. 'Angela only married me for…?'

Her mother, aware of all the details of Rufus's marriage and divorce, had thought it best if they never talked about it, and now Gabriella had thrown it in Rufus's own face!

But he had insulted her mother, for goodness' sake, and his accusations were totally untrue. There was no way her mother could have had debts of a hundred thousand pounds!

She shook her head. 'Not all women are like Angela—'

'Aren't they?' Rufus cut in confrontationally. 'Do you deny the fact that you've done nothing but throw yourself at me for the last year?'

Her cheeks burned at his obvious derision; she was still slightly dazed by the way he had turned on her after the physical intimacy they had just shared.

And, yes, she had been unashamedly besotted with him for the last year, from the very first moment she'd seen him, in fact, but that was because she had fallen in love with him, not for the reason he seemed to be implying.

Implying?

After the things he had accused her mother of he wasn't implying anything, was clearly stating that her only interest in him was the same as her gold-digging mother's had been where his father was concerned—his millions!

Rufus eyed her derisively. 'Do you deny that you also stayed here deliberately today with the idea of seducing me?'

Gabriella knew she couldn't deny that either, but that was only because—because—

Because he had remained totally immune to all her other attempts to show him how much in love with him she was!

And now she knew the reason he had remained immune—because he believed her mother had only married his father for his money, and believed she only wanted him for the same reason!

She shook her head firmly. 'I don't believe a word you've said about my mother.'

'Then ask her, Gabriella,' he challenged scathingly. 'Just

ask her.' He gave a mocking shake of his head. 'I have no idea why my father bothered to marry Heather at all when he was already paying for it—' Rufus broke off abruptly as Gabriella's hand landed hard against his cheek.

Rufus reached up and grasped her wrist, his face dangerously close to hers now, his eyes glowing with an icy heat, the mark of Gabriella's hand starting to show red on one rigid cheek. 'Do that again, Gabriella, and I promise you'll regret it,' he grated between clenched teeth.

Her eyes blazed deeply purple as she glared right back at him, breathing hard in her agitation. 'I hate you!'

'Good,' he said with satisfaction. 'Perhaps in future this will teach you to leave me out of your quest for a rich husband!'

'I wouldn't come near you again if you were the last man on earth!' she assured him emotionally.

'How original!' Rufus scorned.

'You bastard!' Gabriella told him with feeling. 'You're an absolute bastard and I hate you!' She turned and ran into the villa.

Rufus stood poised on the edge of the pool for several furious minutes before turning sharply and diving deep into the water, relishing the coolness as he began to swim the length of the pool.

Gabriella hated him.

Good.

So why didn't it feel as satisfying as he'd imagined?

CHAPTER ONE

FIVE years later, as she gazed across the lawyer's office at Rufus Gabriella knew that she still hated him!

'If I could get straight on to the terms of Mr Gresham's will…?' David Brewster prompted politely once they were seated.

'Go ahead,' Rufus instructed tersely.

He didn't want her here, Gabriella knew. Or his cousin Toby, if the way the two men had greeted each other a few minutes ago was anything to go by. On that she could agree with him however, after what Toby had done.

But although she knew Rufus wouldn't believe her, she really wished she weren't here.

Given a choice, she would rather James hadn't died at all. She'd much rather he were still here giving her the fatherly advice and love that she had found so invaluable since her mother's death a year ago.

James had been devastated after Heather was killed in a car crash last year, and never really seemed to fully recover from the blow. He had suffered a heart attack six months later, and then another, fatal one, a month ago.

No, given a choice Gabriella would rather have had both James and Heather still alive than being summoned to this lawyer's office—as must Rufus and Toby have been—at this time, on this day, for a meeting about James's will.

She and Rufus hadn't spoken at all since they had arrived separately. As they hadn't spoken for the last five years. As they wouldn't ever speak again once this last link with James was severed.

David Brewster's expression was grave as he opened the official-looking document on top of his desk to look at them over the top of the half-moon glasses he had perched on top of his nose. 'First things first,' he said slowly. 'I have already informed by letter the recipients of small bequests in Mr Gresham's will, members of the household staff and suchlike,' he dismissed. 'And there is, of course, a trust fund for his granddaughter Holly, to be administered by her father and myself until she is of an age to receive the bulk capital.'

'Lucky old Holly,' Toby said cheerfully, an actor by profession, his dark good looks unfortunately not matched in talent, meaning that he was very often 'resting' rather than actually working. 'Pity she isn't eighteen rather than seven, then I could have married her!'

'Over my dead body!' Rufus growled in response.

'If necessary,' Toby came back tauntingly.

Gabriella barely listened to the exchange, her earlier tension rising to an unbearable pitch as David Brewster dismissed so lightly those 'small bequests'.

What did that mean?

That she was a recipient of a large bequest…?

If so, Rufus was just going to dislike her more than ever. If that were possible!

Rufus's gaze narrowed on the elderly lawyer. 'Can I ask if this is a recent will of my father's?'

'Indeed it is, Mr Gresham,' the lawyer answered him lightly. 'In fact, it's dated only two months before your father's death.'

Rufus's uneasiness about the contents of his father's will increased.

Of course, that uneasiness could have something to do with the fact that Toby, his disreputable cousin and a constant sponge on James's good will until uncle and nephew had fallen out about three months ago, was also here.

And Gabriella…

He had rarely seen her the last five years, Gabriella having lived and trained as a chef in France for three years after that…incident…in Majorca, and their paths had rarely crossed since she came back to England to live two years ago.

But whenever they had chanced to meet, he had been very aware of the burning intensity of her dislike.

Those five years had done nothing to lessen her beauty, he noted clinically as he looked at her between narrowed lids. In fact if anything she was even more beautiful, none of that youthful eagerness in her face now as she sensed his gaze on her and turned to look at him challengingly.

Her hair was still that gloriously wild cascade of ebony curls loose down her back, but her slenderness was now of almost model-like proportions, her face thinner, too, making those violet-coloured eyes look bigger, her cheeks slightly hollow, her chin more pointed, with only the full, sensual pout of her lips remaining the same.

And he remembered every silken inch of that delectable body, now hidden beneath fitted black trousers and a red gypsy-style blouse that emphasized the fullness of her breasts.

His mouth curled self-derisively as he turned away abruptly, not wanting to dwell on memories of how it had felt to touch her there.

Gabriella saw that scorn on Rufus's face before he turned his attention back to the lawyer, easily able to guess the reason for it. Rufus still believed her to be nothing but a money-grasping little witch.

'Now we come to the reason I asked to speak to you all today,' the lawyer continued briskly. 'Mr Gresham was most specific that I speak to the three of you alone concerning this matter. I'm sure that once I have explained the contents of the will to all of you it will become clear as to the reason why he made that request,' he added ruefully.

Gabriella felt her stomach muscles clench, filled with a terrible premonition.

David Brewster nodded briskly. 'You may read the will for yourselves, but the main provisions are as follows: To his two children, namely Rufus James Gresham and Gabriella Maria Lucia Benito, Mr Gresham leaves the bulk of his estate—some fifty million pounds at the time the will was made—'

'Will you marry me, Gabriella?' Toby put in facetiously.

Gabriella didn't even qualify the question with an answer,

Toby knowing of the complete loathing she felt towards him after he had tried to force himself on her three months ago.

Besides, she was too stunned to do any more than stare disbelievingly at David Brewster!

'If I might continue…?' The lawyer gave Toby a disapproving look above those half-moon glasses. 'All properties, overseas and in England, are to be equally divided between the above-named children, with the exception of the family-owned stores of Gresham's both in England and New York which are to become the property of Rufus James Gresham, at the end of six months, provided that Rufus and Gabriella have lived together in Gresham House for the duration of that time as husband and wife. Those monies and said properties, and all monies owing, will become forfeit to Mr Gresham's nephew, Tobias John Reed, if this above condition is not met— Did you say something, Miss Benito?' the lawyer asked kindly.

Had she groaned out loud? If she had, she hadn't meant to, aware that both Rufus and Toby were now looking at her curiously, too. 'No, nothing,' she quietly assured the elderly lawyer.

But she inwardly cringed, knowing exactly what James meant by 'all monies owing'.

Shortly after her mother's death a year ago Gabriella had attained a bank loan with which to open up her own restaurant, something she had always wanted to do. She had finally felt that she had enough experience to do it, but from the start everything had gone disastrously wrong.

The builder making the alterations on the property she had leased for a year had run way over budget, and then downed tools until she paid up.

There had been a fire in the kitchen prior to opening night meaning that she'd had to hastily—and expensively—bring in new appliances.

And then two months after opening an employee had swindled a customer out of five thousand pounds on their credit card. The customer had refused to be compensated and had sued instead, with the case being reported in all the newspapers, totally tarnishing the reputation of Benito's and closing her down within a month because there had been simply no customers for her to cook for.

All of which had left her with a thirty-thousand-pound loan from the bank, and only the wages from the job she had managed to secure as assistant chef in someone else's bistro with which to pay it.

James had stepped into the breach and rescued her from sure disaster. But only, at Gabriella's insistence, on the condition that they had a legal contract between them that she would eventually pay the money back to him.

A legal contract stating exactly what 'monies' were 'owing'…

And if she didn't live with Rufus as his wife for six months she would owe that money to Toby, of all people. A man she despised even more than she did Rufus.

She glanced across at Rufus beneath lowered lashes, knowing by the expression on that arrogantly handsome face that he definitely hadn't missed her pained groan. And wondered at the reason for it…

Although that emotion was eclipsed by the glittering anger he now directed at her.

'Did you know about this?' he demanded coldly, standing up in restless movements.

Gabriella blinked at his attack, her face very pale, and her violet-coloured eyes so dark they were purple smudges in the pallor. 'I should have guessed you would somehow blame me,' she gasped.

'Who else can I blame?' he came back scathingly. 'My father is beyond recrimination. Leaving you as the only one left with anything to gain by this!' His hands were clenched at his sides.

Never, in all his wildest imaginings, had he believed his father could do something so—so incredibly destructive!

Gabriella gave a hard, humourless laugh. 'You don't seriously think I would ever *choose* to marry you, Rufus!'

Rufus continued to breathe deeply for several long seconds, striving for some sort of control, aware of where they were, of their audience, Toby avidly enjoying the altercation, David Brewster obviously disturbed by it.

And, no, he didn't suppose Gabriella would choose to marry him. Not any more. Not after the way he had deliberately humiliated her in Majorca five years ago.

Deliberately.

Because he never had been as immune to this exotically beautiful woman as he gave the outward impression he was. And her response to him had been mind-blowing, more so than anything he had known before, or since.

But he was always very aware that Gabriella was Heather Benito's daughter, the child of the woman who had taken money from his father before the two of them were even married, and not a small amount, either.

But his father had been so besotted with his second wife, so blind to anything but the fact that he loved Heather, that he had been totally devastated when she had died, to the point that he had almost seemed to cease to function.

Except, it seemed, to write this incredible clause in his will tying Rufus to Gabriella for six months. As her *husband*, for God's sake!

He turned to look at her scathingly. 'Oh, come on, Gabriella,' he taunted. 'We both know to what lengths you're willing to go if you consider the prize big enough!'

Her violet-coloured eyes seemed to burst into flames at his implication. 'You absolute bast—'

'Poor Gabriella,' he scorned. 'Couldn't you have come up with something more original than that in the last five years?'

Her nostrils flared. 'Why bother, when the description fits you so perfectly?'

'Oh, dear.' David Brewster's mild, slightly flustered voice broke into the stormy scene before Rufus could come back with his own cutting reply. 'It would seem that Mr Gresham may have made an error in judgement concerning his wishes for the two of you.'

'Not at all,' Rufus assured the older man grimly. 'My father was fully aware of the—enmity, that exists between Gabriella and myself.'

And James, Rufus knew, had always been deeply saddened at the obviously strained relationship between the two of them.

His father had also advised Rufus numerous times that he ought to remarry, if only to give his now seven-year-old over-indulged daughter a stepmother. A suggestion that Rufus had told him he had no intention of complying with after his experience with Angela.

But James, it seemed, had decided to try and rectify both these situations, after his death, by making this ridiculous condition about Rufus and Gabriella marrying each other in order for them to gain their inheritance.

With the forfeit that Toby would inherit everything instead if they didn't!

Something that James had known that Rufus wouldn't—couldn't—allow to happen. James had held no illusions about the irresponsible Toby, either, and had known that he would ruin Gresham's in a year and have squandered the money away not long after!

The money wasn't important, because Rufus had enough money of his own without needing any of his father's, and the properties in Surrey, Aspen, Majorca and the Bahamas weren't important to him, either. But the two Gresham's stores were different. He had put everything he had into those two stores the last six years, made them more successful than ever, and he refused to let a total wastrel like his cousin Toby just walk in and ruin them.

To the point where he would be willing to marry and live with Gabriella, even for six months, in order to keep them? To live in close proximity with her, day after day, for her to become his wife—something he'd sworn he would never have again! Was he willing to do that…?

'I really had no idea.' The lawyer looked at them frowningly. 'I must admit I thought it rather strange. Nothing I said would deter Mr Gresham from making these particular arrangements in his will, I'm afraid.' He shook his head sadly.

But why wouldn't it? Gabriella questioned, incredulous. What on earth had James hoped to achieve by making such an unacceptable clause in his will?

Because it was unacceptable to both Rufus and Gabriella. As poor David Brewster had just been made a witness to!

Although Rufus now looked self-disgusted that the outburst had been made at all. He was a man who preferred to keep his emotions under control, Gabriella knew. Only she, it seemed, and the prospect of having to marry her, had the power to make him forget that normally cool reserve!

'There has to be some way out of this.' She looked at the lawyer beseechingly.

'I'm afraid not, Miss Benito.' He grimaced. 'I drew Mr Gresham's will up myself, and I can assure you there is no get-out clause, no room for manoeuvre—'

'No two hundred pounds when you pass go,' Toby put in dryly, obviously enjoying this situation immensely.

But then, he would. Toby enjoyed nothing more than dissension and disharmony—even more so if he was the cause of it!

As he had been three months ago…

Which was the reason that forfeit to Toby didn't make any sense to Gabriella. James had been furious with his nephew before he'd died, and wouldn't even have him in the house after what he had tried to do to Gabriella. He certainly wouldn't want Toby to inherit the Gresham's stores, the money, or property.

So why had James put such an ironclad clause in his will…?

Because he *had* known neither Rufus or Gabriella would want Toby to inherit the Gresham's stores, the money or property!

But he also knew that Rufus and Gabriella didn't like each other.

He knew it, but hadn't been happy about it, as he would rather they had all been one big happy family. It was what he had always wanted.

Enough to force Rufus and Gabriella into marrying each other?

A move guaranteed to increase their dislike of each other rather than nullify it!

'What's the matter, Gabriella?' Rufus taunted softly. 'Is marriage to me no longer part of your plans?'

It had never been the plan he was implying it was. She had fallen in love with him six years ago, had loved him five years ago, had thought their being together that day in Majorca had meant that he was in love with her, too. A futile hope, as he had so cruelly pointed out!

Her chin rose to meet his challenge. 'No more than marriage to me has ever been in yours!'

'Not at all, then,' he drawled dismissively.

'Exactly,' she was stung into snapping.

'Isn't this fun?' Toby said to no one in particular. 'Of course, the two of you could just save yourself the trouble of even trying to live together—an exercise obviously doomed to failure before you begin!—and just hand all that lovely loot over to me right now!'

'Miss Benito and Mr Gresham have a week in which to

come to their decision,' David Brewster put in firmly before either Rufus or Gabriella could make a reply.

'Oh, I think I can wait a week.' Toby nodded, totally unperturbed by the animosity surrounding him as he grinned happily.

'There is one other stipulation in Mr Gresham's will that I think you should both be made aware of before coming to that decision.' The lawyer had obviously decided to ignore Toby's comments.

'Let's hear it,' Rufus muttered wearily.

'The two Gresham's stores will, as already stated, at the end of the stipulated six months of marriage become the sole property of my son Rufus James Gresham, but the restaurant within the Gresham's store in London is to be refurbished, renamed Gabriella's, and opened to the public as such and leased in perpetuity to Gabriella Maria Lucia Benito, then to be named Gabriella Gresham.'

Rufus drew in a sharp breath. 'In other words, my father isn't just expecting me to marry and live with Gabriella for six months, he's expecting me to *work* with her, too? Indefinitely!' He spoke with icy control, determined not to give way a second time to the impotent fury he felt, although he could feel a nerve pulsing in his tightly clenched jaw.

'That is so, yes,' David Brewster confirmed ruefully.

'Could I just point out that he's expecting me to live and work with you, too?' an obviously agitated Gabriella put in forcefully.

She hadn't expected that clause in his father's will, either, Rufus acknowledged cynically. She had probably expected to just be able to walk away with her share.

He certainly hadn't missed her involuntary reaction to the mention of 'monies owing' in his father's will. Surely his father hadn't been stupid enough to lend Gabriella money? Money that he must have known would never be repaid?

Rufus looked across at her with cold green eyes, totally unmoved by the pallor in her cheeks. 'I already run Gresham's, already own my own home, already have my own fortune—which one of us stands to gain more here, do you think?'

'You see?' Toby put in again mildly. 'Not a hope in hell of the two of you living together for six months without killing each other! Although,' he added consideringly, 'as that would probably mean that I still inherit—'

'I really don't think those sorts of comments are of any help to this situation whatsoever, Mr Reed,' the lawyer rebuked, obviously having reached the end of his patience. 'I suggest that we meet back here one week from today, at the same time, Miss Benito and Mr Gresham,' the lawyer continued crisply. 'Then the two of you can give me your answer. Your presence will not be needed at that time, Mr Reed,' he added disapprovingly.

They could form a club, Rufus mused hardly.

'There's nothing else in my father's will, no more hidden conditions or clauses,' he prompted hardly, 'that we should be made aware of, is there, before reaching that decision?'

David Brewster met his gaze steadily, seeming to hesitate briefly before answering him. 'No, I can assure you there is nothing further in Mr Gresham's will that concerns any of you,' he said evenly.

'How about the three of us go out to lunch together to talk about this?' Toby suggested brightly as he stood up to leave.

Gabriella knew that any food she tried to eat right now would probably choke her. And just the thought of having lunch with Toby, a man she totally loathed after he had tried to force her into making love with him, made her feel nauseous.

'I think not,' Rufus was the one to answer sharply, surprising Gabriella by taking a steely hold of her arm. 'Gabriella and I obviously have a few things we need to talk about, but, as David has already pointed out, your part in these proceedings is over, Toby,' he added pointedly.

Gabriella looked up at him frowningly. She didn't want to go anywhere with Rufus, either. As for his fingers tightly clasped about her arm...!

Her chin was once again raised determinedly as she tried to break that steely grip. And failed.

Something that made Toby give another unconcerned grin. 'Just let me know when the two of you decide not to get married.'

Married.

The word echoed inside Gabriella's head.

To Rufus.

Just putting the words together—'married' and 'to Rufus'—was enough to send a shiver of alarm down her spine.

But she hadn't always thought so; she would once have been overjoyed at the thought of being Rufus's wife.

Before she'd learnt to hate him.

Before she'd known how much he hated her.

Toby was right; she and Rufus didn't stand a chance of succeeding in living together as husband and wife for six months!

CHAPTER TWO

RUFUS was aware of Gabriella's efforts to shake off his hold on her arm as they left David Brewster's office. A move he had no intention of letting her succeed in making. The two of them needed to talk. Today. Now.

'Goodbye, Toby,' he told the younger man pointedly once they were all outside on the street.

'Don't call us we'll call you?' his cousin came back tauntingly.

Rufus's mouth tightened. He and Toby had never been particularly close, and he knew that James had only tolerated him because he was the son of his only sister. A tolerance that for some reason had come to an abrupt end three months ago.

'Don't hold your breath,' he advised dryly.

Toby gave a derisive laugh. 'Oh, I'll hear from you,' he said with certainty. 'Or Brewster. It really doesn't matter which.' He shrugged. 'The result will be the same.' He grinned confidently.

'Has it ever occurred to you, Toby, that Rufus and I may just both dislike *you* more than we dislike each other?' Gabriella felt stung into replying.

Toby gave her a considering look from insolent blue eyes. 'No,' he finally answered with a mocking smile.

A smile Gabriella would dearly love to slap off his good-looking face!

Her loathing for this man welled uncontrollably. 'Then if I were you, I would start thinking about it,' she advised hardly.

He gave an unconcerned shrug. 'Even if the two of you decide to try this bogus marriage idea, it will never last.'

'We only have to live together for six months,' Gabriella reminded him challengingly.

Toby gave a confident shake of his head. 'I don't think the two of you could spend six hours living in the same house together, let alone six months!'

The fact that he was right only made her angrier. 'You might be surprised!' she snapped, eyes glittering.

'Somehow I doubt it,' Toby dismissed in a bored voice. 'Goodbye, then, Rufus. Ciao, Gabriella,' he added tauntingly before turning to saunter off down the street.

'I was always under the impression that you and Toby liked each other,' Rufus prompted, his gaze narrowed speculatively.

Gabriella looked up at him. 'Impressions can sometimes be deceptive,' she told him huskily, dark lashes sweeping low over creamy cheeks as she hid her thoughts from him.

Not where this woman was concerned, Rufus told himself firmly. She was her mother's daughter, and he had better not ever forget that fact.

His mouth twisted mockingly. 'So is it true that you dislike Toby even more than you dislike me?'

'Oh, yes,' she assured him vehemently.

That had never been Rufus's impression before today, he thought. Gabriella and Toby always seemed to have gravitated to each other in the past whenever there had been any sort of family function. So what had happened to change that?

And did it have anything to do with the fact that his father had also banned Toby from the house three months ago? he wondered shrewdly.

'We need to talk,' he told Gabriella grimly. 'My car is parked—'

'I'm not going anywhere with you,' she instantly protested, taking a step back, forcing Rufus into releasing her this time.

He frowned darkly. 'You know, Gabriella, if we carry on like this then Toby is right—we might just as well hand everything over to him right now!'

Gabriella's eyes widened. He couldn't seriously be thinking about going through with this, could he? With marrying her?

Only with a gun held at his head, she conceded ruefully.

Which was pretty much what James was doing!

'Did I say something amusing, Gabriella?' Rufus snapped as he obviously saw her rueful smile.

No, she acknowledged heavily, her moment of humour over; if anything the joke was on her!

'Not particularly, no,' she sighed. 'But I can't see how the two of us going somewhere to talk is going to make any difference to the fact that we don't want to marry each other.'

'Surely that depends on how we decide to talk?' Rufus came back challengingly.

Gabriella gave him a narrow-eyed glance. The last five years had made Rufus harder and more cynical, the lines of that cynisism etched beside his eyes and mouth, the dark blond hair shorter and the muscled length of his body leaner, but Rufus was still the most breathtakingly handsome man she had ever met.

Nerve-tinglingly so if the way she could still feel his hand on her arm was anything to go by.

An attraction that appeared not to have diminished over the years as she had thought…!

Rufus met her startled gaze, knowing as he did so that he hadn't forgotten a single thing about touching her so intimately five years ago. Or the feel of her slender hands as she had caressed him…

He had been lost the moment he had touched her slender curves, unable to stop touching her until he had taken her over the edge of pleasure, watching her as he had done so, the heat in his own body longing for that same release.

But it was a release he had denied himself, knowing that he couldn't—daren't!—lose himself in her silken warmth, that to do so would be to enter a madness he wouldn't be able to withdraw from.

As he also knew now, every particle of him alive to Gabriella's sensual beauty, that a part of him had continued to want her ever since…

'If you're suggesting what I think you are, then forget it!' Gabriella glared up at him accusingly, her cheeks suffused with colour.

From anger? he wondered. Or something else…?

'Pity,' he drawled mockingly. 'It might have been—interesting, talking over old times.'

'We don't have any "old times" to talk about,' she assured him determinedly.

'No.' He gave a derisive smile. 'What we have to talk about is the future,' he added hardly. 'And we do need to do that, Gabriella,' he said firmly as she would have protested. 'Perhaps come to some sort of—compromise,' he added grimly.

Compromise had never been a word he had associated with thoughts of Gabriella—it was either all or nothing. And until today he had chosen nothing.

Why had his father put that clause in his will?

What possible good could come from forcing the two of them into living as husband and wife, even for six months?

But his father wasn't here to answer those questions, which only left the two of them to find those answers for themselves.

'Compromise…?' Gabriella echoed warily.

She obviously hadn't associated that word with him before, either, Rufus acknowledged ruefully. But it was something they were going to have to find if they weren't both to lose everything. And he didn't seriously believe Gabriella was willing to lose twenty-five million pounds just because she wasn't willing to marry him and live with him for six months to get it!

His mouth twisted derisively as a couple holding hands, obviously deeply in love if the way they gazed into each other's eyes was anything to go by, stepped around them as they stood in the middle of the pavement. 'I really think you're going to have to come back to Gresham's with me, Gabriella, because I have no intention of continuing this conversation in the middle of a public street.'

Gresham's? Gabriella frowned. Why on earth did Rufus want to take her to Gresham's?

She hadn't been in the store since before she had moved to France as she'd been very aware of the fact that Rufus had his office on the sixth floor, and could walk onto one of the shop floors at any given moment. She hadn't wanted to risk even the slightest chance of accidentally bumping into him.

'I have something I would like to show you,' he added throatily.

'Really?' she came back sceptically.

He nodded. 'I think you might be impressed.'

Her gaze narrowed at his deliberate provocation. 'I wasn't last time,' she came back tartly.

'No?' He raised mocking dark blond brows. 'That's not the way I remember it.'

She very much doubted that Rufus remembered their time together in Majorca at all, knowing from James's worried conversations over the years that Rufus had been involved with numerous women since his divorce six years ago. None of those relationships had been of any duration, but she was sure they certainly made his brief encounter with an over-eager eighteen-year-old completely forgettable.

She gave him a saccharin-sweet smile. 'I believe it's called selective memory!'

'Maybe. But which one of us is being selective?' he came back mockingly.

She should know by now not to engage in verbal confrontation with Rufus. He was just too cynical, too much in control, for her to ever be able to win.

Rufus gave an impatient sigh, this sparring with Gabriella achieving nothing but heightening his awareness of her. Something he could quite well do without at the moment.

'I actually thought you might want to take a look at what is going to become Gabriella's,' he bit out harshly, the thought of Gabriella working in the restaurant, two floors down from his own office, not exactly conducive to a calm working environment.

In fact, none of the simpler emotions came to mind when he thought of Gabriella!

Her eyes widened. 'You aren't seriously thinking of complying with the conditions in your father's will?'

'Aren't you?' he came back derisively, Gabriella not resisting this time as he took a light hold of her arm in order to cross the road to where his car was parked.

Rufus was absolutely positive that there was no way this woman would give up the chance to get her hands on that twenty-five million pounds. She was just playing hard to get, or perhaps she thought she could make a separate deal with him, knowing the money wasn't what he was interested in.

His mouth twisted with distaste as he unlocked the Mercedes for them to get into, deliberately not touching Gabriella again as he moved round to get in behind the wheel.

Was she thinking of marrying him? Gabriella wondered with a frown as she sat in the car next to Rufus, both of them silent as he drove to Gresham's.

Her immediate answer was no.

A more considered answer was maybe.

Being married to Rufus was the very last thing she wanted, but the alternative was that Toby inherited everything, including her thirty-thousand-pound debt. A debt she couldn't repay, and Toby, being the warped individual that he was, would probably demand repayment for it in a way that was totally unacceptable to her.

More unacceptable than marrying Rufus?

Most definitely.

'Having second thoughts?' Rufus taunted at her lengthy silence.

And third, and fourth, ones!

She didn't doubt for a moment that being married to Rufus, even short term, would be a living nightmare. She knew that he would take every opportunity he could to make her life a misery, and would naturally assume her compliance meant she only wanted to inherit her half of the fifty million pounds.

But the alternative to that loveless marriage was being indebted to Toby.

At least the nightmare of being married to Rufus would have an end.

'I'm—thinking, about it,' she admitted huskily.

'I thought you might,' Rufus came back bitterly.

'Not for the reason you're thinking,' she snapped impatiently.

'No?' He quirked dark blond brows.

Gabriella didn't even bother to try and defend herself. What was the point? Rufus enjoyed thinking the worst of her, so why disillusion him? Even if she could!

Gabriella had forgotten how good it felt to enter Gresham's, as the doorman in his black uniform jumped to attention to open the door for them as soon as he recognized Rufus. Entering the huge store was to be assailed by exotic smells and sights; it was a feast for the senses, with hundreds of customers being efficiently and warmly served by the dozens of sales staff with items from the food hall to exclusive handbags, to furniture, glasswear, and even a grand piano. Gabriella's eyes glowed with pleasure as she and Rufus walked through the store to the private lift on one side of the ground floor.

For a few minutes, thinking only of the possibilities of opening up a restaurant in this exclusive store, she had totally forgotten the reason she and Rufus were here!

'You don't need me to tell you what an excellent store this is, or how well you run it,' she bit out dismissively.

Rufus eyed her speculatively. 'I was always surprised by your own choice of career...' he murmured questioningly.

She stiffened defensively. 'Why?'

He shrugged broad shoulders. 'Obviously a restaurant in Gresham's would only be open the same hours as the store, but usually restaurant work involves long, unsociable hours.'

Gabriella still eyed him challengingly. 'Your point being?'

His point being that it seemed a career too much like hard work for a woman who had always had her eye on attaining a rich husband...

But maybe she really had thought the way to a man's heart was through his stomach...?

He could have told her years ago that it was usually another part of a man's anatomy that governed his decisions!

Whatever. If they went through with this, after six months Gabriella would no longer have any need for a husband, rich or otherwise.

He shrugged broad shoulders. 'You'll have to cook a meal for me some time,' he said dryly.

Gabriella eyed him impatiently. 'You would be taking a risk—I might be tempted to add arsenic to it!'

'Oh, I'd make you eat some first,' he assured her as they stepped out of the lift onto the fourth floor.

Gabriella gave what was obviously a totally impulsive laugh, her violet eyes glowing, her teeth white and even against the fullness of her lips.

Rufus found himself fascinated by that smile, and stared down at her with hungry eyes.

The laugh caught at the back of Gabriella's throat as she saw the way Rufus was looking at her. Almost as if it were her he would like to eat!

But she must have been mistaken, she decided as that cynicism hardened his face once more, green eyes pale and assessing now as he returned her gaze challengingly.

'Rufus, what—?' She broke off as she realized where he had brought her, her eyes widening and pulse leaping as she looked excitedly round the huge restaurant area on the fourth floor.

A restaurant that, if she agreed to marry Rufus, would become hers. Hers to keep even when the marriage was over.

The restaurant was at the front of the store, taking up half the fourth floor, totally separate from the book and magazine department that took up the rest of the floor space. At the moment it was being run more as a self-service cafeteria, but the possibilities for it becoming an exclusive lunch-time restaurant, as well as a place for morning coffee and afternoon tea, were endless. Gabriella was already able to envisage the changes she would make to the décor, like taking away some of the tables and replacing the utilitarian chairs with more comfortable upright armchairs.

It would become somewhere to relax and enjoy a leisurely lunch that Gabriella would make from totally fresh ingredients—

It could only become that if she agreed to marry Rufus!

'Let's go up to my office and finish discussing this, Gabriella,' he said briskly, once again taking a firm hold of her arm.

Finish discussing it? She wasn't aware that they had started!

Gabriella was familiar with the executive offices on the sixth floor, and indeed the chairman's—Rufus's—plush office, having visited her mother there very occasionally over the period she had worked as James's secretary.

God, that seemed a lifetime ago!

Which, in fact, it was in a way—with her mother and James both gone now, and only Rufus left to torment her.

She didn't recognize the secretary behind the desk in the outer office—but then, why should she?—a tall, shapely blonde who turned to smile warmly at Rufus as the two of them entered the room, and Gabriella gave Rufus a speculative look.

His fingers tightened painfully on her arm as he all but dragged her into the inner office to shut the door firmly behind them. 'I would never make the same mistake my father did,' he assured her coldly as he released her so suddenly Gabriella almost lost her balance.

Never fall in love with his secretary, Gabriella knew he meant. Certainly never marry her.

'They were happy together, Rufus,' she defended impatiently. 'Couldn't you see that? Feel that when you were with them?'

Oh, yes, he had seen his father's happiness with Heather, and knew that losing her had probably killed him. But he believed his father had been blinded by love and had never allowed himself to get close enough to Heather to hear her side of the story, truthful or not.

Heather had certainly tried to get closer to him over the years, but only for his father's sake, Rufus felt sure.

Anyway, Rufus had totally resisted Heather's friendship for his own sake as much as anything else.

Heather and Gabriella, despite Gabriella's years in France, had continued to be close, and if Rufus had lowered his guard towards Heather then he would have been lowering it towards Gabriella, too. And that was something he had no intention of doing.

Either then.

Or now.

He might be being forced into marrying Gabriella if he wanted to keep Gresham's, but that didn't mean he had to like it!

'Did you ever take my advice?' he prompted dryly.

Gabriella frowned her puzzlement at this sudden change of subject, not sure what advice he was talking about.

Rufus's mouth twisted mockingly as he enlightened her. 'Did you ever ask your mother why, six years ago, she needed a hundred thousand pounds?'

Gabriella froze at the taunt, knowing Rufus had done this deliberately, and that he intended to hurt.

Her chin rose challengingly. 'Yes, I did.'

'And?' he prompted impatiently.

And she had promised her mother she would never tell anyone else about it. James had known, of course, because Heather had told him all about her first husband's gambling, and the debts he had left behind for his widow and young daughter. But Heather had wanted to keep that particular skeleton of the Benito family in the closet where it belonged.

'And it's none of your damned business!' Gabriella told Rufus with hard dismissal, having no more intention of sharing that secret with him than her mother had.

'Right,' he accepted scornfully. 'So how much did you owe my father when he died, Gabriella? More, or less, than he gave to your mother all those years ago?'

This time she felt the colour drain from her cheeks.

So Rufus hadn't missed her completely instinctive response in David Brewster's office as he covered that part of his father's will. Or failed to guess the reason for it.

But she should have known that he wouldn't. Rufus was too astute, too intelligent, to fail to guess the cause of her dismayed groan.

'Less,' she sighed, knowing there was no point in prevaricating, Rufus only had to ask David Brewster the same question for the lawyer to produce the contract that Gabriella and James had signed over a year ago. 'Much less.'

Rufus looked at her through narrowed lids. Until that moment he had hoped, had really hoped, that his guess had been wrong. It would have at least been something to know Gabriella hadn't used his father in the same way her mother had.

He should have known better!

'And are you going to tell me exactly why it is you now dislike Toby even more than you dislike me?' he prompted in a scathingly cold voice.

No, she wasn't.

Obviously James had known of Toby's unprovoked sexual attack on her, and the fact that he had changed his will only two months before his death meant it had coloured the way he'd worded that will. But that didn't mean that Rufus was entitled to know about it, too. Besides, with the opinion Rufus had of her, he would probably think she had encouraged Toby's attentions!

'Almost impossible to believe, isn't it, Rufus?' she retorted instead.

He gave a humourless smile. 'About as hard to believe as the claim you once made about not being interested in my father or me because of the money!'

She gave a rueful shake of her head. 'This is never going to work, is it—?'

'On the contrary,' Rufus cut in firmly, moving behind his desk to sit down. If he didn't he might just reach out and strangle her! 'It would at least be a marriage—of short duration, thank God!—based on no illusions whatsoever.'

'On either side!' she came back defensively.

Rufus gave a terse inclination of his head. 'On either side,' he conceded hardly.

Would they really be able to do this? Gabriella wondered achingly.

Somehow she doubted it.

'What about Holly?' she prompted slowly.

Rufus frowned darkly. 'What about her?'

Gabriella grimaced. 'How do you think she will like the idea of living with a stepmother? Even for six months?'

'You would hardly be that,' Rufus assured her scathingly.

'Legally—'

'Stay away from my daughter, Gabriella,' he warned softly.

Her eyes widened; what was he implying? 'And exactly how am I supposed to do that if we're all living together at Gresham House?'

'I suggest you find a way,' he advised hardly. 'The less contact Holly has with a manipulative little money-grasper like you, the better I'll like it!'

He wasn't just trying to wound now, he intended to lacerate and make her bleed, by stating that he didn't even consider her suitable company for his seven-year-old daughter.

'You'll regret this, Rufus!' she struck out instinctively, her eyes glittering deeply violet.

'I already do,' he assured her wearily. 'But I'm sure you will agree that, ultimately, neither of us has any real choice but to go ahead with this bogus marriage?'

Rufus because he had no intention of losing Gresham's to a man like Toby.

Gabriella because she would never allow herself to become financially indebted to a man like Toby, either!

Rufus's mouth twisted at her hesitation. 'Just say yes or no to marriage, Gabriella,' he rasped scathingly.

She felt like a mesmerized rabbit caught in the headlights

of an oncoming car. She drew in a shaky breath. 'Yes,' she bit out. 'We both know my answer has to be yes!' she added shakily. Six months. That was all she would have to live with him for. Surely she could survive that…?

'Just as mine has to be.' Rufus nodded abruptly. 'Although I want to make it absolutely clear that marriage to you is the last thing that I actually want!' he added insultingly.

Her eyes flashed deeply blue. 'It's the last thing I want, too!'

He nodded again. 'As long as we're both aware of that. Now, if you wouldn't mind?' he added firmly. 'Some of us have work to do.'

She had work to do, too, and needed to get to the bistro in time for the six o'clock opening. Not that she would be working there much longer once she and Rufus were married.

She would be too busy in the next few weeks preparing and then opening the restaurant downstairs.

That was some consolation.

Not a great one, but it would give her something else to concentrate on other than being married to Rufus.

As if she really would be able to think of anything else…!

CHAPTER THREE

THERE were four people present at their wedding ten days later; Rufus and Gabriella obviously, plus David Brewster and his politely smiling secretary as their two witnesses.

The ceremony was over so quickly Gabriella was sure she couldn't really be married to Rufus at all, feeling more than a little dazed as Rufus complied with the invitation to kiss the bride.

She hadn't been this close to Rufus since that day five years ago, and to her despair she was lost from the moment his mouth claimed hers. It wasn't a light brush of the lips as she'd expected; instead Rufus took her fully into his arms to explore her mouth with a thoroughness that took her breath away.

His eyes glittered defiantly as he at last raised his head, and the fact that he looked totally unmoved by the intimacy, while Gabriella felt as if every nerve in her body had come tinglingly alive, was enough for her to meet his challenge with an icy stare.

'Yes. Well.' A slightly flustered David Brewster spoke awkwardly beside them. 'Perhaps it's time we were going...?'

Perhaps it was, Rufus allowed, his heart thumping in his chest, another part of his body knowing the same surging beat.

Damn it, he had kissed Gabriella just to see what would happen. An experiment, to see if her ebony-haired beauty, and the sensual pout of her mouth, could still stir him.

The answer was a resounding yes.

His own mouth tightened and his eyes narrowed briefly on hers, before he turned to face the elderly lawyer. 'I want to thank you and Celia for coming with us today.' He bestowed a warm smile on the middle-aged secretary. 'For obvious reasons, it wouldn't have been fair to involve any of our friends.'

Speak for yourself, Gabriella brooded; she, for one, could have done with a friend at her side today.

'Perhaps I could take the two of you out for a celebration lunch…?' David Brewster suggested as they moved out into the reception area of the register office where Gabriella and Rufus had just been married.

'I—'

'That won't be possible, I'm afraid,' Rufus refused for both of them. 'I have to get back to work, and I'm sure Gabriella is going to be busy moving the rest of her things into Gresham House.'

She knew the crack about moving the rest of her things into Gresham House was a direct attack on the fact that, seeing no reason to keep paying the rent on her apartment when she wouldn't be returning there at the end of the six months, she had given notice and moved some of her things to Gresham House and put the rest into storage until she needed them again.

'Another time, perhaps,' David Brewster accepted lightly.

Rufus gave a mocking smile. 'Oh, I don't think that Gabriella and I will be getting married again any time soon!' he taunted.

'To each other or anyone else!' she came back impatiently.

Although she had no idea why she should feel that way. This was a short-term marriage of convenience, so why should it bother her that Rufus was dealing with their wedding as just another piece of business completed?

'Exactly,' he drawled. 'Now—' He broke off as they stepped outside to find a barrage of cameras clicking and flashing in their faces and at the same time a babble of questions being fired at them. 'What the—?' He scowled darkly at the photographers and reporters as he said a hasty farewell to David Brewster and his secretary and took a firm grasp of Gabriella's arm to pull her with him towards where his car was parked, totally ignoring the questions as he did so.

But it was impossible not to hear them…!

'How long have you and Miss Benito been involved?'

'Where are you going on honeymoon?'

'Did your father know the two of you were getting married before he died?'

'Miss Benito, did you—?'

'Her name is now Mrs Gresham,' Rufus snapped coldly, having already bundled Gabriella into the passenger seat. Getting in behind the wheel, he started the engine, absolutely furious, his expression grim as he tried to manoeuvre his car through the throng of press still surrounding the car.

'Don't look at me!' Gabriella protested as Rufus turned to give her a frustrated glare. 'As if I would tell anyone we were getting married!'

But she doubted that Rufus had, either. David Brewster's discretion could also be relied on, she was sure, as could his secretary's, so who—?

'Toby!' Rufus verbally came to the same conclusion as her mental puzzling had taken her.

Yes, Gabriella realized, it had to be Toby, knowing alerting the press to their wedding would be his idea of fun!

'How did he know we were getting married today?' Rufus grated as they at last escaped the reporters and he was able to get out into the flow of traffic.

'Well, I can assure you that I didn't tell him,' Gabriella told him determinedly, still a little surprised—and disturbed—by the fact that Rufus had kissed her after the wedding service.

'So much for keeping this quiet,' Rufus muttered grimly. 'I can just see the headlines in tomorrow's newspapers; "GRESHAM HEIRS MARRY"! Followed by, "The bride wore cream"—'

'Buttermilk,' Gabriella corrected dryly.

'I'm a man, okay,' Rufus turned to snap impatiently. 'It just looks cream to me!'

Buttermilk, the woman in the shop had described it as being when Gabriella had bought the dress earlier in the week, having decided that although this wasn't a proper marriage, she should at least make an effort to wear something new for the service.

Rufus, wearing a dark grey suit, white shirt, and grey tie, just looked as if he had come straight from the office.

Which, indeed, it turned out he had!

Making Gabriella feel glad she hadn't gone to the bother of getting flowers, too.

'Just drop me off at a train station,' she told him woodenly. 'I can get a train back to Gresham House.' The reality of what they had just done was beginning to sink in, and a quiet train ride away from Rufus would give her a bit of space to think.

She hadn't realized she would feel like this about the wedding. She'd just imagined it as being a formality she had to get out of the way before gritting her teeth and getting through the next six months.

Of course, Rufus had been married before, so this wedding probably brought back a lot of unhappy memories for him, as well as new ones.

It had all seemed so logical when Rufus had made the arrangements. So cool. So calculated. Something to be got through.

A little like a trip to the dentist!

Now all Gabriella could think of was that this wasn't the wedding her mother had always dreamt of for her. And those thoughts of her mother, who would never be here to witness Gabriella's real wedding, when or if it happened, only made her want to cry.

Rufus gave Gabriella a sideways glance. Were they tears he could see glistening in the smoky violet depths of her eyes?

No, he decided harshly after a second look, it was more likely a glitter of triumph than tears. Not only was she going to inherit half the Gresham millions, but Rufus had been forced into the inconvenience of marrying her at the same time!

Suitable vengeance indeed for what he had done to her five years ago.

He turned his attention back to the road, his hands tightly

gripping the steering wheel. 'I thought we might go and have a celebration drink before you leave.' The even tenor of his voice betrayed none of his inner anger with the unpalatable situation.

Not that he hadn't tried to get out of it, having paid a visit to his own lawyer, who had gone into consultation with David Brewster as to whether or not the will could be broken, only to be told that it couldn't, and that David Brewster had done his job very well indeed.

But just because he had been forced into taking Gabriella for his wife didn't mean that she could have things all her own way.

And she was his wife…

'A drink?' she repeated now. 'Are you sure you have the time?' she added sarcastically.

What had she expected, that he would take the day off, that they would drive to the register office together, be showered with confetti and good wishes when they came out, followed by a wedding breakfast at some exclusive hotel for family and friends?

The fewer people who knew about this marriage, the better, as far as he was concerned.

Although the reporters waiting outside the register office just now would probably take care of that.

He would have words with Toby about that at his earliest convenience.

'I can make the time,' Rufus confirmed dryly.

Gabriella gave him a searching look. Was he being kind—something she couldn't believe where she was concerned!—or did he have another motive for wanting to spend more time with her?

He probably just wanted to give her another lecture about staying away from his daughter!

Holly would be seven years old now, and it was over five years since Gabriella had actually spoken to her. She had seen the little girl at a couple of family functions since, so she knew that she now looked exactly like Rufus, with her toffee-coloured hair and pale green eyes, but other than that Gabriella had no real knowledge of the little girl whose mother had walked out of her life when she was only a couple of months old, never to return.

That had to have been hard on Holly.

Gabriella could only hope that the little girl wouldn't consider her the equivalent of a wicked stepmother. Although, according to Rufus, Holly was to be involved in this bogus marriage as little as possible.

'Okay,' she sighed, not in any particular hurry to return to Gresham House, where the housekeeper and the rest of the staff were no doubt preparing for the arrival of the new Mr and Mrs Gresham!

'Try and sound a little more enthusiastic, Gabriella,' Rufus taunted softly. 'After all, this is our wedding day.'

'Don't remind me!' she came back tartly.

Rufus gave a derisive smile. He didn't need any reminding of the fact she was now his wife, either.

Gabriella looked a little alarmed when he parked the car and guided her over to a tall apartment building. 'Where are you taking me?'

'I keep an apartment here for whenever I'm delayed in town on business,' he dismissed lightly, nodding to the security man on the desk before stepping into the lift and pressing the numbered security code for the top floor.

Whenever he was delayed in town on business, Gabriella echoed silently with a frown. What did that mean?

That he kept an apartment in town for when he wanted to spend the night with one of his women?

He couldn't exactly take a stream of women back to the house he shared with Holly, now could he? He'd have to have somewhere more private for those—relationships.

And he was taking her there…

'I don't think this is a good idea, Rufus—' But she didn't get any further with her protest as Rufus pulled her close against his body, his head lowering as his mouth claimed hers.

Yes, she definitely tasted good, Rufus acknowledged distractedly as his mouth captured and plundered hers. And no doubt the rest of her was going to taste just as delectable, too.

At this moment he wanted Gabriella with a driving need he had no intention of keeping under control. Gabriella was now his wife and he intended touching and tasting every glorious inch of her.

What was Rufus doing? Gabriella barely had time to wonder before she became lost in the pleasure of the hunger of his mouth moving searchingly against hers, his tongue now caressing lightly along her bottom lip before surging into her mouth, setting a sensuous rhythm that caused a fire between her sensitive thighs.

She groaned a low murmur of capitulation as his hands moved up to capture the proud tilt of her breasts, his thumbs caressing the already hardened nipples, stroking the sensitive tips until she pressed closer against him, wanting, wanting—

She gasped as she felt her breasts released from her dress. She hadn't even been aware of Rufus undoing the tiny buttons down the front, and there was only the thin silk of her camisole now between her thrusting breasts and the warm caress of his hands.

He dragged his mouth from hers, trailing fire down the column of her throat, holding her hands against her waist as he bent his head to claim one aching nipple through the silky material, sucking gently as his tongue moved over it in sensual demand.

She should stop him, knew in her maturity exactly where this was going, but there was no way, absolutely no way, even with that knowledge, that she could fight the emotions Rufus was arousing in her, and her back arched impulsively as his tongue flicked against her.

Gabriella clung to him weakly, completely lost at this unexpected assault on her senses, the unaccustomed ache between her thighs building to an unbearable pitch.

The lift doors opened straight into the penthouse apartment with a gentle swish, cool air washing over them, Gabriella quivering slightly as that air brushed the damp material of her camisole.

She opened pleasure-drugged eyes as Rufus raised his head to look at her, the last five years swept away in that single moment of mutual desire.

Gabriella simply didn't want this pleasure to stop! She couldn't stop it!

Rufus stood her beside the bed, slipping the dress down her arms and letting it fall to the floor before sitting her on the side of the bed and standing back to look at her dressed only in the cream camisole and matching silk panties.

'Take off your top,' he instructed huskily as he took off his jacket and dropped it to the carpeted floor beside her dress.

She wasn't eighteen any more, but a mature woman of twenty-three, and, although she was still not experienced like Rufus, she was more than a match for Rufus's overt sensuality.

Gabriella held his gaze with hers as she moved a shaking hand to slide first one silky strap of her camisole down her arms and then the other, the material falling down to her waist, her dark-tipped breasts thrusting proudly forward, begging for his touch.

He knelt down between her legs as he moved forward to lick her nipples into harder arousal, deliberately teasing first one, and then the other. Gabriella leant into him as she silently asked for what would drive her completely over the edge.

Rufus had no doubts that this time he would go with her, would take his fill, would keep her here with him until he had taken her in every way, given her every pleasure he could think of.

His lips parted and he took the hardened tip of her breast fiercely into his mouth, instantly feeling the shudders that convulsed Gabriella's body. His hand moved to push her panties aside and touch the centre of those pleasurable convulsions, increasing the pleasure as he sought and found the sensitive nub, stroking her to a deeper and stronger climax.

When her shuddering release came to an end he moved

slightly so that he could draw that last silken garment from her body before lowering his head to capture the sweet taste of her.

Gabriella was completely lost, floating in a sea of sensual pleasure, her eyes dazed as Rufus stood up to look down at her, completely and unashamedly naked, knowing she wanted him, all of him, inside her.

'Help me undress, Gabriella,' he encouraged throatily.

She felt a nervous fluttering in her stomach, a nervousness she instantly dismissed. She was a woman now, no longer a besotted teenager, and she expected nothing more from Rufus than the physical pleasure he could, and did, give her. A physical pleasure she intended returning.

She held his gaze with hers as she slowly unbuttoned and slipped the silk shirt from his shoulders, and then trailed her hands down the length of his chest and across his stomach. She heard his slight catch of breath as one of her hands settled on the fastening of his trousers, that breath released in a sharp hiss as she slowly slid the zip down before moving her hand against his hardness, pure instinct governing her actions now as she began to pleasure him as he had pleasured her.

His hands became entangled in her hair. 'No, Gabriella!' he gasped. 'I want to be inside you. Deep inside you,' he grated before dropping to the carpeted floor and taking her with him.

Beneath her. Pulling her on top of him. His eyes were dark as he looked up at her, arching into her as he slowly lowered her onto the long length of him, his hands reaching up to caress her aching breasts as she began to move in rhythm to his thrusts.

Gabriella ignored the initial stinging pain as Rufus entered her, and leant forward so that he could capture one hardened nipple in his mouth. She felt her own pleasure deepening, and spiralling out of control once again as Rufus kissed first one breast and then the other, all the time moving his body into hers, with his hands on her hips helping to guide her movements.

Rufus's hands closed tightly against her when he could hold back no longer and his release began, taking her with him as they both reached a shuddering climax that seemed to rip them asunder before joining them again, making them one.

Gabriella lay collapsed on Rufus's chest in the aftermath, their bodies slick with sweat, but soon she could feel herself tensing as she waited for the words of scorn, the mockery that was sure to come for her uninhibited response to him.

Instead there was only the sound of their ragged breathing in the otherwise silent room, steadying to a rasp, before settling into normality.

Why didn't Rufus say something? Gabriella wondered.

Where were the accusations?

The recriminations?

Even though he had been the one to start all this, kissing and touching her in the lift on the way up here, knowing Rufus as she did she was sure he'd twist this around somehow so that she was the one who had seduced him.

As far as Rufus was concerned she had always been the one responsible for their physical encounters.

Except that this time they were married to each other…

'It looks, Gabriella, as if when the time is up we'll have to get a divorce rather than an annulment.' He suddenly spoke derisively, his own thoughts obviously on their recent marriage, too.

She raised her head slowly to look at him, the tangled length of her silky hair falling over her shoulders down onto his chest. 'What do you mean?' she asked.

He smiled up at her, a hard, almost wolfish grin. 'Merely that now I have such a sexy little hell-cat for a wife I won't need to use this apartment again for six months.' He flexed his shoulder where the marks of her teeth could still be seen. 'Unless, of course, you want to come here occasionally, for a bit of variety?'

In other words, now that they were married, Rufus intended to use her in the same way he did his mistresses—purely for recreational sex...

Gabriella didn't think so!

CHAPTER FOUR

'WHERE the hell did you disappear to this afternoon?'

Gabriella looked at Rufus's reflection in the bathroom mirror as he stood behind her in the doorway, and felt grateful that he hadn't arrived seconds ago before she had wrapped a towel around her after her shower. She wasn't sure she could have dealt with talking to him while completely naked!

Not that he really needed an answer to his question; it must have been pretty obvious to Rufus that she had taken the opportunity of his going to take a shower to make good her escape from the apartment. The apartment where they had just made love. The apartment where Rufus took all his mistresses, it seemed…

He hadn't exactly chased after her, had he? Seven o'clock, she had been informed by her scornful new stepdaughter, was 'the usual time Daddy came home from work'. And it was just after seven now.

Gabriella made no effort to turn and look at him, preferring to look at his reflection in the mirror instead. She picked up a bottle of her favourite scented lotion, and tipped some into her hands before smoothing it over her arms.

'I thought we had finished with each other for the day,' she said derisively.

His mouth twisted. 'Did you? Or did you just run out like the little coward that you are?'

'Would you please leave my bathroom, Rufus?' she said coldly, her eyes challenging as she looked up to find him watching her movements, his gaze dark with a desire she had no intention of acknowledging. 'Your rooms are further down the hallway, I believe.'

He leant nonchalantly against the doorframe. 'And what are you going to do if I don't leave? Call for help?'

Probably a futile gesture, she acknowledged; he was the new master of the house, after all...

But then, it also reasoned that she was the new mistress of the house, too. 'If necessary,' she confirmed coolly, smoothing the scented lotion over her shoulders now.

Rufus drew in a ragged breath, deeply irritated by her coldness after the pleasure they had shared that afternoon. Gabriella had been like fire in his arms earlier, totally wanton and abandoned. Why the sudden change?

If they were to live together for six months, then Rufus fully intended to share his wife's bed for that length of time! Considering her behaviour in Majorca, and her response to him today, he had thought she would want the same.

Gabriella certainly couldn't claim she wasn't attracted to him.

So why, earlier this afternoon, when they had just enjoyed each other so much, had she taken advantage of his brief absence to disappear back here to Gresham House?

'I asked you to leave, Rufus,' she repeated coldly, not even looking at him but concentrating on rubbing lotion onto the creamy swell at the top of her breasts now.

Breasts he wanted to kiss and caress as he took her once again with the wild abandon of earlier today that had driven him completely out of his mind.

Her long dark hair was secured loosely on top of her head, exposing the vulnerable column of her throat and shoulders, her skin creamy and soft, skin he—

She glanced up at him irritably as she obviously sensed his heated gaze. 'Still here?'

He drew in a harsh breath. 'I live here, too!'

'And as I've already said, your bathroom and bedroom are further down the hallway,' she snapped.

'Perhaps I like this one better than mine?' he taunted.

'In that case we can swap rooms.' She shrugged.

This was a different Gabriella from the one Rufus had previously known, different from both the eager teenager five years ago, and the woman who had been so wild in his arms this afternoon. This was a cooler, more self-contained Gabriella.

'I've been informed that dinner is at eight o'clock,' he bit out tersely.

Gabriella gave a cool inclination of her head. 'That's the time I instructed the housekeeper earlier.'

Rufus gave a humourless smile. 'You don't mind taking on some of your wifely duties, then!'

She continued to look at him steadily. 'Some of them.' She gave a gracious inclination of her head. 'But I'll choose for myself which ones they will be, Rufus,' she added firmly.

Sharing his bed for the next six months wasn't one she 'chose' to take on, apparently.

Damn!

This afternoon it had seemed the perfect solution to the constant hunger he had to possess her. It would be a mutual satisfaction that required no commitment from either of them, no false promises, and would give him exactly what he wanted when he wanted it.

Gabriella in his bed.

Having her now play hard to get didn't fit in with that idea at all.

'Shouldn't you be going to see Holly now?' Gabriella prompted pointedly. 'She informed me when I spoke to her earlier that you always spend half an hour with her before she goes to bed.'

Rufus frowned darkly as he straightened. 'Do I sense criticism in your voice, Gabriella?'

'I don't know—do you?' she came back softly, coolly holding the reflection of his pale green gaze with hers.

Inside she trembled, the memories of their lovemaking clearly etched in her mind, remembering how she had completely lost control in Rufus's arms.

It should never have happened, but it had been so unexpected, so instant, that she simply hadn't had the strength or will-power to resist knowing Rufus intimately to see if she still felt that same desire for him.

Which she did. More than ever, it seemed...

But by giving in to that weakness she had put herself in a vulnerable position from the onset of this bogus marriage, a position she intended reversing as quickly, and abruptly, as possible. By whatever means possible.

Rufus's mouth thinned. 'My relationship with my daughter is none of your damned business!'

She raised her dark brows. 'Do you have one?'

His gaze narrowed. 'And exactly what is that supposed to mean?'

Gabriella turned to face him, scornful now. 'Spending half an hour with her every evening can hardly be called a relationship!'

Gabriella remembered her own early school years with affection. Her mother waiting outside the school gates to walk home with her. The two of them then sitting down together at the kitchen table enjoying a cup of hot chocolate as they chatted over the events of the day. Her mother helping her with her homework before they cooked the evening meal together.

Of course that had changed slightly once the two of them had been left on their own and her mother had had to work full-time to support the two of them. But Gabriella had been older then, almost fourteen, and quite capable of looking after herself until her mother came home, having a meal ready for her mother when she came in from work, as she had usually been too tired to feel much like doing it herself. It was how Gabriella had discovered her own love of cooking.

Holly Gresham was seven years old, was taken to and brought home from school in a chauffeur-driven car, when she was then given her tea in the kitchen with the cook. Holly wasn't old enough to have homework yet, but seemed to spend her time after tea in her bedroom anyway. Until her father came home. And then the two of them spent that 'half an hour together' before she went to bed.

Holly had haughtily informed her of this earlier when Gabriella had knocked on her bedroom door to see what she was doing.

Holly was definitely her father's daughter. She seemed to have inherited all of his arrogance and self-containment, and didn't appear to mind the hours she spent alone in her bedroom, or the fact that she bathed herself before preparing for bed. At the age of seven she already gave the impression of needing no one.

But as far as Gabriella was concerned, Holly was far too mature and serious for a seven-year-old.

Gabriella accepted that it couldn't have been easy for Rufus to have been left with a two-month-old daughter. After all, he'd had a job to do, responsibilities, and initially had had to engage nannies to care for his baby girl, only dispensing with them when Holly had begun school two years ago. But from the amount of expensive toys that now filled Holly's bedroom, Rufus seemed to have showered his motherless daughter with material objects rather than the love and time with him she really needed.

His relationship with his daughter was none of Gabriella's damned business, Rufus had informed her, and for the short time she would be in their lives maybe it wasn't, but that didn't stop her from having an opinion.

Or from informing Rufus of that opinion.

Something, from the dark anger on his face, he didn't appreciate at all…

'I told you to stay away from Holly,' he bit out hardly.

Gabriella shrugged bare shoulders. 'I thought someone should check earlier whether she was alive or dead—'

'You have no right, damn it—'

'Besides,' she continued firmly, 'I was never particularly fond of being told what I can and can't do.'

Rufus scowled. 'Then perhaps it's time you learnt—'

'Are you threatening me, Rufus?' she cut in.

He stared at her for several long moments, filled with frustrated anger that she had dared to criticise the way he was bringing up his own daughter.

'No, I'm not threatening you, Gabriella,' he finally murmured softly. 'I'm merely surprised that I'm receiving parental criticism from a woman whose own mother was nothing but a—'

'I advise you to stop right there, Rufus.' The ice in Gabriella's voice was definitely genuine this time, her chin raised in warning as she looked at him with sparkling violet eyes. 'I tell you what, Rufus, how about we make a deal?' she continued scathingly. 'You leave my mother out of this and I won't comment on your own deficiencies where parental guidance and care for your daughter are concerned, either— how does that sound?'

Like a backhanded insult, Rufus realized with a frown.

Six months of sharing a house with this woman were going to seem much longer than that!

Gabriella picked up her watch where she had taken it off before her shower, glancing down at it pointedly. 'If you don't leave now you won't have time to spend that half an hour with Holly before dinner.'

'Do I take it that you'll be in for dinner this evening, too?' He raised dark blond brows, deciding to ignore the intended criticism this time. Gabriella was spoiling for a fight, and he didn't have time for it right now.

'And why wouldn't I be?' she came back tartly.

Rufus shrugged. 'I thought you worked in a bistro or something in the evenings?'

'Not any more,' she dismissed. 'I finished working at the bistro yesterday, Rufus. As from Monday I shall be starting the refurbishment to Gabriella's,' she reminded him sweetly.

Damn! After everything that had happened today he had forgotten he would be sharing a workplace with her, too!

'The minutes are ticking away, Rufus,' she said tauntingly. 'You really shouldn't keep Holly waiting.'

Toby had been right, Rufus told himself angrily as he turned and walked away; he wasn't sure he was going to be able to stand six hours in the same house as Gabriella, let alone six months!

'Where's your wedding ring?'

Gabriella looked across the dinner table at Rufus with deliberate coolness as the two of them sat in the small family dining-room where their dinner had been served fifteen minutes earlier. Not that either of them had eaten too much so far, the melon starter having been sent back almost untouched, the salmon not faring much better. Gabriella had no idea why Rufus wasn't eating, but she was far too aware of him sitting opposite her to be able to eat.

She had thought this situation through before coming

downstairs for dinner, knowing that after this afternoon she had to retrench, and had decided that cool was how she had to be to deal with Rufus in future. If nothing else it stopped him from reading her other emotions, and it had the added bonus of infuriating him at the same time!

Her anger got her nowhere because Rufus simply turned it back on her. And he could be much more insulting than she ever could!

Being pleasant just wasn't an option after Rufus's suggestion earlier today that they could share a bed—and their bodies—for the next six months.

And ignoring him was a complete non-starter when she was so aware of him!

So she was left with cool. Which was actually quite hard work when she was naturally gregarious and chatty.

But anything she chatted to Rufus about he was likely to turn back on her, so she had simply decided not to talk to him unless he spoke to her directly.

As now.

'I took the ring off earlier when I had a shower,' she answered dismissively. 'I didn't want my finger to turn green!'

Besides, it felt like a dead weight of ownership on her finger...

'And what the hell is that supposed to mean?' he demanded incredulously, putting down his knife and fork to look at her. 'Do you think I've given you some cheap piece of metal and glass as a wedding ring—is that it?'

Her eyes widened. 'You aren't telling me the diamonds and gold are real?'

They hadn't actually talked about exchanging rings during the wedding service—they hadn't really talked about anything much at all in the ten days before the wedding, with Gabriella just receiving telephone instructions from Rufus as to when and where. So she had been a little surprised when Rufus had produced the thin gold-coloured band studded with what she had assumed were pieces of glass, at the appropriate moment in the service, and slipped it on her finger.

'You're saying they are real?' she repeated with a frown as Rufus continued to look at her disbelievingly.

They made a strange newly married couple, she was sure, sitting politely across the dinner table from each other, both having dressed for dinner, with Gabriella in a fitted black knee-length dress and Rufus in a formal shirt and trousers.

She had made the effort more for the sake of the household staff than she had for Rufus, and she was sure he had done the same; after all, neither of them was particularly interested in impressing the other!

'Well, of course they're real,' Rufus came back impatiently. 'Do you honestly think I would give my wife an imitation ring?'

'Why not? It's an imitation marriage!' she dismissed. 'Or is it just that Rufus Gresham couldn't be seen to give his wife an imitation ring?' she scorned.

She was still spoiling for a fight, Rufus decided. And he would still like nothing better than to oblige. But at the same time, he didn't feel much like giving Gabriella anything she wanted tonight…

'That about sums it up.' He nodded. 'I only asked,

Gabriella. Do what you like with the damned thing.' He shrugged, resuming eating his salmon.

Two could play this particular game. But they would play by his rules or not at all.

'How was Holly?' Gabriella prompted after a couple of minutes' silence.

'Fine,' he dismissed tersely. 'Still a little bemused by the fact that her aunt Gabriella is now her stepmother, but, other than that, just fine,' he added with a steely edge to his voice.

'Perhaps you shouldn't have told her—'

'Oh, yes—' Rufus gave an impatient sigh '—you would rather she found out when some unsuspecting member of the household staff turned around and called you Mrs Gresham, is that it?'

Gabriella put her knife and fork carefully down on her plate, picked up her napkin and delicately pressed it against her lips before answering him. 'The household staff all call me Miss Gabriella,' she told him evenly. 'I trust you told Holly that the stepmother thing is only a temporary arrangement? That it won't interfere at all with your own—relationship, with her?'

God, he hoped they weren't going to have too many dinners alone like this—he wasn't sure his digestion could take it!

He put his own knife and fork down noisily on his plate this time, the salmon, like Gabriella's, only half eaten. 'I'm not in the habit of explaining myself,' he bit out tautly.

She gave a cool inclination of her head. 'To anyone, it seems.'

'Oh, to hell with this!' He threw his napkin on the table before standing up. 'Thank goodness I'm going to New York next month for a few days—it can't come soon enough for me!'

Outwardly Gabriella remained unmoved by his outburst, but inwardly she was plagued by totally differing emotions. She was relieved that his totally disturbing presence was to be removed for several days. And she was dismayed at the hollow feeling in the pit of her stomach at the thought of his not being here for the same length of time.

She was relieved, she told herself firmly. That feeling in the pit of her stomach was merely indigestion from having to try to be polite to him at the same time as she was trying to eat.

That was all it was.

'Well?' he challenged, looming large in the small room. 'Don't you have a comment to make about that, too?'

She met his angry gaze straight on. 'Have a good trip…?'

He drew in a deeply controlling breath as he continued to glare down at her, knowing she was deliberately baiting him. 'I meant with regard to Holly!'

She grimaced. 'But you've told me not to make any more comments about your relationship with your daughter.'

'And I take it this is one of those occasions where you choose to do as you've been told?'

'Exactly!' she confirmed sweetly.

Rufus gave an impatient shake of his head, badly needing to get out of here. Before he shook her rather than his head! This certainly wasn't his usual time of relaxation at home after a day at work. Gabriella had him wound up so tight he was in danger of exploding. And, as he knew from past experience, that explosion could take many forms.

'Maybe there will be some sort of emergency that will keep me in New York for a month instead of a few days!' he bit out forcefully. 'It would be four weeks less that I would have to try living in the same house as you!'

Not by so much as the twitch of a facial muscle did Gabriella show that his remark wounded.

Because why should it?

She had known from the onset that the last thing Rufus wanted to do was share a house with her, to be married to her, so why should she care when all he was doing was once again verbally confirming those feelings?

She cared because of what had happened between them this afternoon...

She really hadn't expected to end up in bed with Rufus immediately after their wedding. In fact, it had been the very last thing she had expected to happen. But now that it had, she couldn't get it out of her mind.

They had been hungry, ravenous for each other, the moment they had stepped into the lift. In fact, they had barely made it to the bedroom at all before ripping each other's clothes off!

And it had been totally different from what had happened in Majorca. Then she had been full of girlish expectations, and had been hopelessly in love.

This afternoon, despite the fact that it had been the first time for her, their lovemaking had been wild, uninhibited, and totally adult.

What scared her was that it could happen again at any time.

And what scared her even more was that it wouldn't!

How ridiculous was that?

Rufus continued to look at her for several long seconds

through narrowed lids, his gaze piercing, as if trying to see the thoughts behind her violet-blue eyes.

Gabriella withstood his look for as long as she could, her own gaze cool, her expression still coldly challenging.

Luckily it was long enough, with Rufus giving a disgusted snort before turning to leave.

'Oh, and Rufus…?' She stopped him at the door.

He drew in a deeply controlling breath before slowly turning back to look at her. 'Yes?'

'I should hang onto the apartment, if I were you,' she advised derisively. 'For the future use of you and—whoever!'

So that he had no doubts whatsoever that she wouldn't be the one sharing that bed with him again!

His pale green eyes glittered with angry need to retaliate as he glared down at her. 'I'll do that,' he finally bit out mockingly. 'For my future use with—whoever…' he added with soft challenge before turning and striding forcefully from the room.

Gabriella heard a door slam further down the hallway seconds later, and could only presume he had gone to the room that used to be his father's study, but was now his…

She collapsed weakly down in her chair now that she was alone, at last giving into the bewilderment she had felt ever since leaving his apartment.

She hadn't been able to get out of there fast enough, after it had hit her what she had done. And she certainly had no intention of letting Rufus know he had been her first and only lover.

She didn't want him to ever know that.

CHAPTER FIVE

'EXACTLY what are you supposed to be doing?'

Gabriella wobbled slightly at the top of the stepladder she was standing on, only just managing to keep her balance before turning to look down at Rufus as he stood at the bottom of the ladder staring up at her with critical eyes.

She probably looked a mess, Gabriella acknowledged with an inward cringe. Her hair was tied back with a scarf but several tendrils had come loose to fall wispily about a face flushed and hot from her exertions. A face bare of make-up. And her purple tee shirt and black denims were looking a little the worse for wear, too, from where she had been removing paintings and dusty artificial plants from around the coffee-shop all morning. There was probably a smudge of dirt on her nose, too, knowing her luck!

Whereas Rufus looked wonderful, as usual, in the dark business suit and cream shirt with matching tie he had worn in to work today.

Not that Gabriella had known that until now—the two of them had travelled separately into town this morning,

Gabriella waiting until Rufus had left to drive himself to Gresham's before catching a train, and this was the first time she had seen him since she'd arrived a couple of hours ago.

'What does it look like I'm doing?' she came back impatiently as she carefully made her way down the stepladder.

Losing her balance and falling into Rufus's arms was the last thing she wanted to do after keeping him at arm's length the whole weekend.

Not that it had been all that difficult to do!

Rufus, whether from habit, or because of Gabriella's criticism Friday evening—or simply a desire to keep Holly safely away from her—had taken Holly into work with him on Saturday and then out for the day on Sunday, the two of them not arriving back at Gresham House until after dinner on both evenings, Rufus then putting Holly to bed before disappearing into the study for the rest of the evening.

Leaving Gabriella to spend a very lonely weekend rattling around Gresham House on her own, a house definitely meant to hold a very large family rather than one lone, bored female.

'I thought you said you were getting workmen in to deal with the refurbishment to the restaurant?' Rufus frowned darkly. Gabriella was obviously working here alone, as sheets had been put up to cover in the area, and a closed notice outside with the announcement that Gabriella's would be opening in two weeks' time.

That 'closed' notice, as far as Rufus was concerned, did not apply to him.

'So I am.' She reached the bottom of the ladder, dusting her hands together as she did so. 'They're starting tomorrow. But

I thought I could do the preparation work myself, taking down all the old artwork and such,' she dismissed with a shrug. 'And I hate plastic plants.' She wrinkled her nose delicately.

'You prefer the real thing, do you?' he mocked.

Gabriella met his gaze steadily. 'In everything, yes.'

He hadn't even been aware she was in the building until a member of his senior staff had mentioned the fact that it was good to see the work had started on the new restaurant.

He had resisted coming down to see for himself for at least—oh, half an hour or so, fighting down the restless need he had to see Gabriella again.

She looked beautiful, Rufus acknowledged irritably, even as he saw by the stack of paintings and false potted plants that she must have been working for some time.

Her hair, that glorious abundance of ebony curls, was hidden beneath a purple scarf, and her eyes glowed the same colour, framed by lashes long and sweeping. There was an almost luminous glow to her creamy cheeks, just the slightest smudge of dirt on her nose, and her purple tee shirt clung lovingly to the curve of her breasts, and also allowed a glimpse of bare midriff above the low-waisted denims that showed off the long length of her legs.

He had deliberately taken Holly out for most of the weekend, half as a need to get completely away from Gabriella, the other half, he had recognized disgustedly, a need to punish her for not having the same physical need for him as he was undoubtedly developing for her.

A need that was, after only a few days of living together, driving him insane.

Quietly.

Achingly.

Completely insane!

And now she was here at Gresham's, too, looking more desirable than ever even without the sophistication of make-up and smart clothes.

'I prefer the real thing, too,' he said, challenge in his voice. 'It's a pity it's often so hard to find.'

'Keep looking, Rufus,' she derided. 'I'm sure you'll find it one day!'

'Maybe I don't want to find it,' he came back dismissively.

She shrugged. 'Your choice.'

Yes, it was, and after Angela he had known only too well what artifice was. Gabriella's mother had only confirmed his opinion of women! Now Gabriella used her desirability in exactly the same way.

And *still* he wanted her!

He grimaced self-derisively. 'One of the staff mentioned you were here and I thought you would probably want to come upstairs to the senior management dining-room for your lunch?'

Gabriella looked up at him and frowned, not quite trusting the invitation. After all, he hadn't exactly shown any consideration for her welfare over the weekend, now, had he?

Her brow cleared as she found the answer, her smile derisive. 'Do you think your staff will expect you to put on a show of newly married bliss, too, Rufus?' she taunted, knowing that there couldn't be a Gresham's employee who wasn't aware of the fact that the two of them had been married last Friday.

The newspapers on Saturday morning, as Rufus had expected, had been full of the story, several of the tabloids actually having their photograph on the front page, one screaming that headline, GRESHAM HEIRS MARRY, just as he had predicted, too. The reporter—obviously also male—hadn't recognized the colour of her dress as buttermilk, either!

But they had been a one-day wonder, thank goodness, with yet another government scandal taking over the headlines in the Sunday newspapers.

His mouth tightened. 'I'm sure that my staff, as you put it, are too discreet to comment on our marriage at all!' Although he had received several good wishes and congratulations himself this morning when he'd walked through the store.

'It is a little hard to believe, isn't it?' Gabriella came back with dry dismissal.

Rufus wondered if she knew how arousing this constant need she had to fight with him actually was, as it kept alive the constant flame of sexual awareness between them. Probably not. She wouldn't be doing it otherwise!

He gave an impatient sigh. 'I made the suggestion about lunch, Gabriella, because I think it would appear odd if you didn't eat in the same place as your husband.'

Her grin was of pure malevolence. 'That must be a little hard for you to accept, Rufus!'

'Not at all,' he came back smoothly. 'But you might want to—freshen up, a little,' he drawled mockingly, 'before joining the rest of us upstairs.'

Gabriella waited until he had strolled away before sticking

her tongue out at his broad back. A childish gesture, maybe, but it made her feel—

'I'm sure if we gave it some thought we could find a better use for your tongue, Gabriella,' he drawled huskily without turning, lifting up one of the surrounding sheets before disappearing back out into the main store.

—like an idiot! Gabriella acknowledged frustratedly.

She sat down heavily on the bottom step of the ladder, breathing deeply, knowing she had definitely lost that round!

Which was one of the reasons she deliberately delayed going upstairs to the executive dining-room for half an hour, taking Rufus's advice and tidying herself up first, removing the scarf from her hair before brushing it silkily about her shoulders, giving her face a quick wash, and brushing the worst of the dust from her clothes.

Besides, the longer she delayed, the more chance she had of Rufus having eaten his lunch and already returned to his own office.

No such luck, she realized the moment she entered the dining-room and saw Rufus seated at a table with what she presumed were several of his department managers.

The seat beside him having been left conspicuously empty…

For her, presumably.

As his wife.

Hmm…

'Sorry I was delayed, darling,' she told him huskily as she kissed him lingeringly on the lips before sitting in the chair next to him, her expression deliberately bland as he studied her with his pale green eyes between narrowed lids.

'That's okay—darling,' he came back just as deliberately. 'I know how busy you are.'

She gave him a provocative smile. 'But not so busy I don't have time to have lunch with my husband. Aren't you going to introduce me, Rufus?' She looked pointedly at the other people seated at the table, five of them, and all of them studying her with avid interest.

Rufus made the necessary introductions, pretty sure that Gabriella wouldn't remember half the names by the time they had finished eating.

He was also aware that Gabriella was enjoying playing with him.

On the basis that she thought she had him at a disadvantage in front of his managers?

He turned slightly in his seat so that the length of his thigh came to rest against hers, the slight instinctive movement she gave away from that touch showing him that she wasn't as coolly immune to him as she liked to pretend she was.

'Mmm, you smell lovely, darling,' he breathed throatily as he brushed her lips with his.

Gabriella drew back, eyeing him uncertainly now. 'I didn't know you were partial to eau-de-dust, darling,' she muttered warily now as yet another ploy to hit out at Rufus seemed to be backfiring on her.

Rufus moved back slightly, his smile taunting as he gazed down at her. 'You always smell good to me, Gabriella,' he assured her as he lifted the weight of her hair to nuzzle against her ear.

A move she definitely wasn't expecting! Somehow Rufus

had never come over to her as a man who would be demonstrably affectionate in public—in fact, she'd thought he'd be the opposite.

Especially with a woman he would rather not even have as his wife—

'I should stop while you're not ahead, Gabriella,' he took the opportunity to rasp warningly against her ear before straightening in his seat, looking for all the world as if he were pleased to have her sitting beside him.

So much for her decision on Friday night to remain cool whenever she was with him, she berated herself as she distractedly ordered a chicken salad for her lunch, definitely feeling hot and flustered.

And not just from their verbal sparring, either. Her lips still tingled from his unexpected kiss, and her earlobe felt highly sensitized, too, just from the brush of his warm breath.

Cool? She was so physically aware of him she felt hot all over!

Which wasn't conducive to her having an appetite to actually eat her chicken salad when it arrived, especially as Rufus kept the long length of his thigh pressed against her leg all through the meal, seemingly unaware of the contact himself as he talked business with his managers.

She would have moved away from him if she could, but other than getting far too near to the man sitting on her other side—something that would look decidedly odd in a newly married woman—she had no choice but to suffer that crippling closeness.

Rufus's gaze was full of laughter as he turned to look at her. 'Not eating your salad, darling?' he chided softly as she pushed the plate away with almost as much food on it as when she'd started. 'You really have no need to diet; you're thin enough already.'

Her lack of appetite had nothing to do with dieting—and he knew it didn't.

She gave him a saccharin-sweet smile. 'I don't seem to have any appetite for food, Rufus—I think I must be in love!'

Rufus met the challenge in her eyes as he moved to drape an arm over the slenderness of her shoulders. 'Perhaps we should have gone away on a long, long honeymoon now rather than delaying it until the summer?' he drawled huskily.

Honeymoon? Days and nights alone with Rufus? She didn't think so!

That suggestion certainly had her defences up, Rufus recognized, Gabriella's shoulders feeling extremely tense beneath his arm.

But it had occurred to him a few minutes ago that the two of them being at work only a couple of days after their wedding must look a little odd to the rest of the staff at Gresham's…

He hadn't quite expected this tangible response from Gabriella to the suggestion of a honeymoon, though…

'I think I had better be getting back to work now,' Gabriella announced lightly as she casually—but very definitely—shook off the weight of his arm. 'It was nice to meet you, Patrick, May, Jeff, Nigel, and Jan.' Her smile encompassed all of them as she stood up.

Rufus was amazed that she had remembered all the managers' names after all. Not only that, but she had looked at each of them in turn as she'd said their name.

'I'll come down with you,' Rufus said firmly as he stood up beside her.

She shot him a startled glance. 'Don't let me break up your meeting.'

'It was over, anyway,' Rufus dismissed with a shrug, his arm about the slenderness of her waist as he guided her through the dining-room.

In fact, he couldn't even remember what had been discussed! This woman, he realized, totally addled his mental faculties. And totally heightened his physical ones.

'Everyone is staring,' she muttered uncomfortably.

Rufus smiled at one of the staring before answering her. 'The men are just looking at me enviously.'

'And I suppose the women are looking at me the same way?' she came back tartly.

He turned to give her a wolfish grin. 'Maybe.'

They probably were, Gabriella acknowledged impatiently. Rufus, with that deep blond hair, rugged good looks, and a natural sexual appeal, was by far the most handsome and charismatic man in the room. And the fact that he was the owner of the whole building probably didn't hurt, either.

Although there was one part of the building he didn't have control over, she remembered with satisfaction. Even when this sham of a marriage was over she would still have the restaurant Gabriella's.

'What are you smiling so smugly about?' Rufus prompted suspiciously.

She looked at him with deceptively innocent eyes. 'I was just wondering what your senior staff would say about their oh-so-proper boss if they knew that immediately after our wedding you couldn't even wait to get out of the lift before starting to rip my clothes off!' she taunted.

'Like this lift, you mean?' he retorted as the doors to his private lift opened with a swish.

Ah. Perhaps this wasn't the time—or the place—for her to have used that particular incident to mock him!

She grimaced. 'I think I'll just walk down, after all. It's only two floors.'

Rufus gave a husky laugh. 'Scared of a replay, Gabriella?'

'I need the exercise,' she told him determinedly.

Rufus looked at her, frowning. That was certainly not true. She really was much thinner than she had been five years ago, with the slenderness only making the pert shape of her breasts more prominent. Breasts he was sure were completely naked beneath her purple tee shirt!

He had been well aware of this fact as he'd tried to talk sales and displays with his managers, her breasts actually brushing against his arm once as Gabriella had leant forward to pick up the salt pot.

'In that case, so do I.' He nodded.

She blinked her uncertainty. 'Rufus—'

'Just walk down the damn stairs, Gabriella,' he rasped. 'What is so difficult about that?'

There was nothing difficult about walking down the stairs, it was the intent in those glittering green eyes that bothered her!

'Don't you have any work to do?' she said tartly.

He shrugged. 'Nothing that can't wait.'

Gabriella was fast getting to the stage where she couldn't

wait. The close proximity with Rufus for the last hour had heightened all her senses, and made her totally aware of his every movement, of the taut leanness of his body, of a need for that mocking mouth to possess hers.

This physical attraction and fascination she had for Rufus were unlike anything she had ever known, and were totally beyond her control.

And they shouldn't be!

She knew Rufus's opinion of her only too well—she should do, he reminded her of it often enough! But that seemed to make no difference to this total physical awareness she had of him, her skin seeming to tingle just at the touch of his hand on her elbow as they walked down the stairs together.

She was breathing hard, and not from the exertion of descending the stairs. Her face felt flushed and feverish, as every nerve, every inch of her sang with a desire that she could feel rapidly escalating out of control.

Rufus could sense Gabriella's increasing tension as he maintained that firm grip on her elbow, giving her a sideways glance as he wondered at the reason for it.

Her eyes were glowing, her cheeks were flushed, and her nipples were pressing against her tee shirt in full arousal.

Dear God…!

He waited only long enough for them to enter the precarious privacy of the restaurant before pulling her into his arms and claiming her full, pouting mouth, while Gabriella met the fierceness of his kiss with a hunger of her own.

Her hands were everywhere, under his jacket, moving restlessly across his back before returning to unbutton his shirt, her fingers against his heated flesh now, and her nails digging into him in a caress that only increased the throb of his desire.

Rufus wanted to devour her, and he gave in to that need as he pushed her tee shirt out of the way, wrenching his mouth from hers as he bent his head to take one of her nipples into his mouth.

Gabriella groaned with pleasure, her fingers entangled in his thick blond hair as she held Rufus against her, the flick of his tongue against her taut nipple sending her into shuddering paroxysms of pleasure.

'Not here, Rufus,' she groaned as he opened the button on her denims and slowly began to slide the zip down. 'There are people in the bookshop...!' she protested weakly as her insides melted when she felt his hand hot against her abdomen.

His lips released her as he moved up to look down at her. 'I have to!' he told her achingly. 'I have to, Gabriella!' he repeated with a fierce ache, kissing her as he manoeuvred her against the wall, one of his hands capturing her breast and teasing the nipple as his other hand slipped downwards, beneath her panties.

Gabriella was lost the moment his fingers touched her, parted her, and found the roused centre of her, caressing, stroking, and filling her with heat.

Wave after wave of pleasure gripped her, shaking her foundations as she clung to Rufus's shoulders for support, and she bit her bottom lip in an effort not to cry out as her release went on and on, convulsing around him.

'Yes, Gabriella! God, yes...!' Rufus raised his head to encourage throatily as she flamed in his arms, totally enjoying the feel of her pleasure, the taste of her, her head now arched back as she gave in to the pulsing pleasure.

His arms moved about her as, those quaking emotions finally quietening to a low throb, her legs gave way beneath her. Her face was flushed, her eyes dark and unfocused, and her hair a wild cascade of ebony curls that he longed to bury his face in.

'Gabriella—'

'I can hear someone!' Gabriella gasped in panic as she tensed, that wild release still making her tremble, her senses heightened to feel, colour, and sound.

And, even if Rufus wasn't aware of it, she could hear the purposeful click of someone's shoes on the marble walkway as they headed through the book section in this direction.

She pulled away from him, not daring to even look at Rufus as she straightened her tee shirt and buttoned up her denims with shaking fingers.

She couldn't believe what had just happened between them, the utter madness of what they had just done.

They were in the middle of Gresham's, for goodness' sake!

Anyone looking at them, at Rufus's tousled blond hair, the colour high against his cheekbones, the fullness of his arousal—and no doubt her own disorderly appearance—would know exactly what they had just been doing!

She had just managed to make some sort of semblance of order to her clothing, and Rufus had buttoned his shirt and straightened his tie, when the sheet was pushed aside and Rufus's secretary entered, her expression politely enquiring.

If she sensed or saw anything amiss she didn't show it by

so much as the blink of an eyelid, although her smile was slightly apologetic. 'I'm sorry to disturb you, Mr Gresham, but the deputy manager of the New York store has been on the telephone. He needs you to call him back urgently.' She directed that apologetic smile at Gabriella, too, now.

Gabriella felt decidedly uncomfortable, guessing that the other woman knew exactly what she had interrupted!

Mortifying!

Although Rufus, to give him his due, looked totally unconcerned. 'I'll be there in a few minutes, Stacy,' he dismissed.

'We're all greatly looking forward to seeing the new restaurant you're opening, Mrs Gresham,' she told Gabriella warmly.

'Thank you,' she accepted huskily, deciding she liked Rufus's secretary, after all.

Anyone who could remain this friendly as well as efficient when confronted with two people who had obviously recently been in the throes of passion had to be okay!

Although Gabriella wasn't so sure about being called Mrs Gresham...

'I'll make the call and come back, Gabriella,' Rufus told her huskily once they were alone again.

To finish what they had started?

It had been madness in the first place, certainly couldn't be expected to continue after this interruption!

She swallowed hard, not quite able to meet Rufus's gaze. 'Perhaps it might be better if we—if we, discussed this at home, later this evening?'

Discussed it?

There was nothing to discuss. They couldn't seem to spend

more than half an hour in each other's company without one or both of them wanting the other.

All the talking in the world wasn't going to change that!

Rufus looked at Gabriella for several long seconds, knowing that for her the moment was over, that reality had set in with a vengeance, her face pale now, her eyes huge violet pools of uncertainty.

He nodded abruptly. 'Until later, then.'

'Yes,' she confirmed huskily, still not quite looking at him.

And he wanted her to look at him, wanted to be completely naked and have her eyes, and then her hands, on him, to caress him, touch him, take him!

And he wanted her in the same way. Touching wasn't enough. He wanted to look at her, too, every silken naked inch of her.

His hand moved to cup her chin as he raised her face to his, looking deeply into her startled eyes. 'We need to talk, Gabriella,' he told her huskily.

She looked even more startled, and then her gaze became wary. 'What about?'

His mouth twisted into a humourless smile. 'This, for one thing.'

By 'this' she knew he meant this totally uncontrollable response they had to each other. And she didn't want to talk about that, could make no sense of it herself with all the animosity there was between them, too, certainly had no way of explaining how she felt to Rufus.

She moved away from that cupping hand, her chin raised in challenge. 'Animal lust, Rufus?' she dismissed hardly.

His mouth thinned even as his eyes narrowed dangerously.

'I have to go, Gabriella,' he rasped. 'But we will talk,' he added warningly before striding off determinedly.

Gabriella waited until he had gone before giving in to the tears she could no longer control.

Because, she realized achingly, she still loved him!

She had been in love with Rufus five years ago, and she was still in love with him now.

How and why didn't seem important, only the fact that she was.

And it was a love that Rufus could no more return now than he had been able to five years ago.

CHAPTER SIX

'So you really went ahead and married him…'

Gabriella turned sharply at the sound of that mocking voice, almost overbalancing as she once again stood on the stepladder.

'Toby,' she greeted scathingly, her gaze narrowing as she looked down at him.

He was his usual rakishly handsome self in faded denims and black tee shirt beneath a brown suede jacket. Yes, Toby was tall, dark, and very handsome—and as usual he left her completely cold.

'What do you want?' she demanded coolly as she came down the stepladder.

'Why, to offer my congratulations, of course,' he drawled derisively. 'And to ask how you're enjoying being married to my dear cousin Rufus!' he added tauntingly.

Her mouth twisted. 'And why would you think I would be interested in telling you anything, about Rufus or anyone else?'

He shrugged unconcernedly. 'Why not?'

'You can ask that?' she snapped, frowning. 'After what you did to me—'

'*Tried* to do to you, Gabriella,' he corrected lightly. 'And was it my fault you decided you weren't interested, after all?'

Her eyes widened. 'I never was interested in you in that way, Toby!' she assured him forcefully.

He gave another shrug. 'My mistake, then,' he dismissed lightly. 'And you can't blame a man for trying.'

'Oh, yes, I can,' she assured him fiercely.

'Why don't you just let bygones be bygones, Gabriella?' he reasoned. 'I can assure you, I've already forgotten it.'

Her eyes widened incredulously. He had forgotten coming to her bedroom three months ago when she had been staying at Gresham House with James for the weekend? He had forgotten kissing her, pushing her back on the bed, trying to force her as he pulled at her clothes and muttered obscenities in her ear?

A scene that James—thank goodness—had walked in on and put an end to! Resulting in him banning Toby from ever entering Gresham House again.

'Get out, Toby,' she ordered shakily. 'Just get out!'

'Wouldn't you like to hear how you can put an end to your marriage to Rufus right now and still get your hands on the twenty-five million?' he prompted as he pulled out a chair and sat down.

Gabriella shook her head. 'I'm not interested in anything you have to say.'

'But you haven't heard—'

'About anything!' she added disgustedly, knowing that whatever Toby was going to propose was sure to mean bad news for someone. In this case, it sounded as if it was probably

The Harlequin Reader Service® — Here's How It Works:

Accepting your 2 free Harlequin Presents® larger print books and 2 free gifts places you under no obligation to buy anything. You may keep the books and gifts and return the shipping statement marked "cancel." If you do not cancel, about a month later we'll send you 6 additional Harlequin Presents larger print books and bill you just $4.05 each in the U.S. or $4.72 each in Canada, plus 25¢ shipping & handling per book and applicable taxes if any.* That's the complete price and — compared to cover prices of $4.75 each in the U.S. and $5.75 each in Canada — it's quite a bargain! You may cancel at any time, but if you choose to continue, every month we'll send you 6 more books, which you may either purchase at the discount price or return to us and cancel your subscription.

*Terms and prices subject to change without notice. Sales tax applicable in N.Y. Canadian residents will be charged applicable provincial taxes and GST. All orders subject to approval. Credit or debit balances in a customer's account(s) may be offset by any other outstanding balance owed by or to the customer. Please allow 4 to 6 weeks for delivery.

If offer card is missing write to:
Harlequin Reader Service, 3010 Walden Ave., P.O. Box 1867, Buffalo, NY 14240-1867.

NO POSTAGE
NECESSARY
IF MAILED
IN THE
UNITED STATES

You'll get
2 FREE
mystery gifts along
with your 2 FREE books!

BUSINESS REPLY MAIL
FIRST-CLASS MAIL   PERMIT NO. 717-003   BUFFALO, NY

POSTAGE WILL BE PAID BY ADDRESSEE

HARLEQUIN READER SERVICE
3010 WALDEN AVE
PO BOX 1867
BUFFALO NY 14240-9952

Would you like to read
Harlequin Presents® novels
with larger print?

ACTUAL TYPE SIZE!

GET 2 FREE LARGER PRINT BOOKS!

Larger Print Editions

Harlequin Presents® novels are now available
in a larger print edition! These books are
complete and unabridged, but the type is larger,
so it's easier on your eyes.

YES! **Please send me 2 FREE *Harlequin
Presents* novels in the larger print format
and 2 FREE mystery gifts! I understand I am
under no obligation to purchase any books,
as explained on the back of this card.**

376 HDL ELYF   176 HDL EL2F

FIRST NAME	LAST NAME

ADDRESS

APT #	CITY

STATE/PROV.	ZIP/POSTAL CODE

Order online at:
www.eHarlequin.com

HLP-P-05/07

DETACH AND MAIL CARD TODAY ▼

Printed in the U.S.A. © 2006 HARLEQUIN ENTERPRISES LTD.
® and ™ are trademarks owned and used by the trademark owner and/or its licensee.

Rufus. 'How did you know Rufus and I were married?' she prompted shrewdly.

Toby shrugged. 'Just a simple telephone call to David Brewster was all it took. He was more than happy to tell me that the two of you were getting married in order to comply with the condition in Uncle James's will.' He grimaced. 'I have the distinct impression that the distinguished lawyer doesn't like or approve of me!'

'I can't imagine why!' Gabriella came back scathingly. 'And I suppose you're the one responsible for the reporters turning up at the register office in that way?' she derided, sure that David Brewster had had no idea how Toby would use his knowledge about the wedding.

'Just a little joke on my part.' Toby shrugged unconcernedly. 'Knowing how you and Rufus feel about each other, I thought it might be fun if there was a photograph of the two of you in the newspapers!'

Gabriella stiffened. 'And how do we feel about each other…?'

'On Rufus's part, obviously utter contempt,' he announced cheerfully. 'And, at a guess, wary distrust on yours.'

Well, he was certainly right about Rufus's feelings towards her.

But totally wrong about her feelings for Rufus!

As she had only recently discovered herself…

'That's really none of your concern, is it, Toby?' she dismissed. 'I believe I asked you to leave?'

'And I believe I told you I have a business proposition for you,' he came back impatiently.

'A business proposition I'm not interested in—'

'Don't say that until you've heard what it is—'

'I don't need to hear what it is!' she assured him hardly. 'Any business proposition that you suggested is sure to be suspect.'

'Very funny!' He sighed his impatience with her obstinacy. 'The thing is, Gabriella, all you have to do is walk out on this marriage to Rufus, defaulting on the six-month condition, and then when I inherit I'll go halves with you.'

He really had it all worked out, didn't he?

'After which the two of us could get married if you want,' he suggested huskily. 'I've always wanted you, Gabriella—'

'I would rather stay married to Rufus—who, as you say, has nothing but contempt for me—than ever marry you!' she gasped incredulously.

'Now that isn't nice, Gabriella,' he murmured as he stood up to take a step towards her.

'Don't come any nearer,' she warned, eyes wide.

'Or else what?' he challenged confidently.

'I'm warning you, Toby!' She glared, having no idea what she was going to do if he didn't stop.

If she shouted for help it would cause a scene, in the middle of Gresham's, for goodness' sake, but there was no way, absolutely no way, she could allow this man to come anywhere near her. He disgusted her as no one else ever had, and seemed to think what had happened three months ago was nothing but a joke.

'What are you going to do, Gabriella?' he taunted. 'There's no Uncle James here to protect you this time.' His face hardened. 'And considering you're the reason he completely disinherited me, I think you might try being a little—nicer to me, than you are.'

Gabriella knew exactly what he meant by 'nicer'. And just the thought of that with this man made her feel ill.

'This is as "nice" as it's going to get, Toby,' she assured him firmly. 'Now you have to leave,' she pleaded shakily, totally disturbed by how close he was to her. 'If Rufus finds you here it's only going to cause trouble.'

'But I want the two of us to be friends again, Gabriella,' he told her persuasively.

They had never been friends, just part of the same family, someone for each of them to talk to on family occasions, and, after the way he had behaved, they didn't even have that any more.

'Rufus could come down here at any moment and find you here,' she insisted—and goodness knew what he was going to think if he did! 'You really do have to go, Toby!'

Toby smiled confidently. 'Rufus doesn't scare me—'

'No?' Rufus challenged icily as he lifted the sheet to enter the restaurant, his hard gaze raking mercilessly over Gabriella and Toby, his closed expression revealing none of his inner feelings at the brief snatch of conversation between them he had just overheard.

Because he wasn't absolutely sure what he had overheard.

Gabriella had been pleading with Toby to leave, but had that been because she'd really wanted him to go, or because she hadn't wanted to risk him finding the two of them here together?

Just because looking at her drove him wild with wanting her—when hadn't it?—was no reason for him to have ever doubted the opinion he had always had of her being a gold-digger.

Just because he could drive her just as wild in bed as she drove him, was no reason for him to think that changed her real motives…

After finding her here with Toby, perhaps it might be as well if he didn't let his own desire for her blind him to that fact!

Toby smiled. 'Give a man a break, Rufus. Gabriella and I were—friends, long before the two of you went through with this bogus marriage. We argued three months ago, that's all, and she's more than a little ticked off with me—enough to marry you, it seems,' he added tauntingly. 'But that's all it is.'

'That's a lie!' Gabriella glared at him. 'Rufus, surely you don't believe what he's saying, do you?' She sighed impatiently.

He didn't know what to believe any more, his own desire for Gabriella having completely clouded his usually clear judgement. And at the moment he was incensed at the way Toby had been standing so close to Gabriella when he'd come in, at the claims he was making of the two of them being involved, both in the past and now.

He gave his cousin a glacial look. 'I think you had better take Gabriella's advice and leave, Toby. And if you want to see—my wife, again, might I suggest you wait another six months before doing so,' he added harshly. 'She'll be richer by twenty-five million then!'

'Rufus, when I've told you how much I dislike him, you can't seriously believe I've ever been involved with Toby?' Gabriella gasped.

But she could see that he did, the slightly more approachable Rufus she had come to know the last few hours replaced with the coldly arrogant adversary who had always enjoyed thinking the worst of her.

How much of her conversation with Toby had he overheard?

Enough to have heard her pleading with Toby to leave before Rufus found him here, obviously. And to have completely misunderstood the reason for her pleading!

But she hadn't been pleading with Toby to leave because she cared about him; she knew only too well that he was quite capable of taking care of himself. But she had feared for the precarious truce she and Rufus seemed to have reached today. Rightly so if the return of his coldly accusing gaze was anything to go by!

She gave a dazed shake of her head. 'Rufus, I would never—'

'Save your breath, Gabriella,' Toby drawled ruefully. 'Can't you see that Rufus doesn't believe a word you're saying?'

Toby was right, Rufus didn't believe her, Gabriella recognized as she looked at him searchingly, his handsome face hard and unyielding as he returned her gaze.

How could she make him see—? How could she make him believe—?

She couldn't!

Because the Rufus she was looking at now didn't want to believe her...

'I think you had better go, Toby,' Rufus told the younger man coldly.

Toby shrugged, unconcerned, his expression mockingly challenging. 'Just give me a call, Gabriella, when you're tired of punishing me for our stupid argument. Just think what the two of us could do with that fifty million pounds once we're married!' he added enticingly. 'Oh, yes, Rufus, I've asked Gabriella to marry me,' he taunted as he saw his cousin's stony expression.

'That might be a little difficult for her to do when she's already married to me,' Rufus grated.

'A marriage easily disposed of,' Toby dismissed confidently. 'And when it is, Gabriella will be my wife.' He smiled. 'You see, Rufus, Gabriella can't lose either way, can she?' he added tauntingly.

'Get out!' Rufus bit out grimly, so furious he wanted to reach out and strangle his cousin.

Or Gabriella.

He didn't really mind which!

Toby eyed him mockingly. 'What are you going to do, keep her tied to the bed for the next six months?'

'If necessary, yes!' Rufus rasped harshly, not even able to look at Gabriella at that moment.

Disappointed didn't really begin to describe how he felt about her.

After seeing the way she had worked so hard clearing out the restaurant this morning, the charm she had exerted over his work colleagues during lunch, and her uninhibited response to him here only minutes later, he had started to wonder if he might not have misjudged her after all.

He had momentarily forgotten that all Gabriella was interested in was her twenty-five million pounds! In fact, if she really was involved with Toby, then Toby was absolutely right; whether she stayed with him or eventually went to Toby, Gabriella was in a win-win situation.

His anger was all the stronger, he knew, because he had started to doubt the opinion he had always had of her.

But not any more. Never again could he allow his physical need of her to overshadow what he knew to be the true Gabriella.

'Still here, Toby?' he dismissed hardly.

His cousin shrugged. 'I thought if I hung around a while I might get to see a bit of genuine wife-beating!'

Gabriella's startled gaze moved sharply to Rufus's rigidly set features, a nerve pulsing in his tightly clenched jaw.

Rufus's mouth tightened to a thin line as he saw the uncertain way Gabriella was looking at him. Damn it, he had never struck a woman in his life, and he certainly wasn't going to start with her. No matter how much she provoked him!

'That may be your way of dealing with things, Toby,' he told his cousin disgustedly. 'But, personally, I abhor physical violence to anyone.'

'Pity.' Toby grinned unconcernedly. 'As I said, Gabriella, just call me when you can't stand being with the pompous bastard a moment longer. I promise I'll be waiting!'

Rufus's hands clenched at his sides as he watched Toby swagger out, taut with tension, knowing that, despite his denial, he was closer to hitting someone at that moment than he had ever been in his life before.

'Rufus—'

'I have no intention of discussing this with you any further just now, Gabriella,' he bit out coldly as he turned back to her, her beauty still as tantalizing, but Rufus was equally determined he would never be tempted again. 'I only came down here to tell you that I have to go to New York for a few days on urgent business.' He gave a disgusted shake of his head. 'Perhaps it's as well if I get away from you for a while!'

Perhaps it was, Gabriella accepted miserably. But she would miss him. And she hated admitting that as much as she hated the fact that Rufus believed she had only confirmed his opinion of her by apparently being involved with Toby.

But in the meantime Rufus would only go on despising her.

And now, knowing that she was still in love with him, it was more than a matter of personal pride that she prove him wrong about her.

'Will you be gone long?' she enquired stiffly.

He looked at her coldly. 'Wifely interest, Gabriella?' he scorned. 'Or do you just want to know how much time Toby will have to—*persuade* you around to his way of thinking, before I get back?'

She shook her head. 'Toby couldn't persuade me to cross the road with him.' She sighed. 'In fact if Toby were the last man on the planet I still wouldn't give him the time of day, let alone agree to marry him,' she added with a shudder of revulsion.

Rufus's eyes narrowed, the disgust in her voice too genuine for it to be a false claim.

'What happened three months ago, Gabriella?' he prompted shrewdly.

She gave him a startled look, all the colour draining from her face. 'Happened…?' she delayed.

He shrugged. 'My father changed his will three months ago

for a reason. Toby claims the two of you argued three months ago. It seems logical to assume the two are connected.'

Logical, yes. Painful—very much so!

She swallowed hard, knowing there was no point in trying to avoid answering him. 'I was staying at Gresham House with James. Toby came on a visit. He—' She drew in a deeply controlling breath. 'He tried to— He came to my bedroom, claimed I had been encouraging him for months, and when I assured him I hadn't he—he tried to force me!'

It had been the most frightening experience of her life. Toby gave every impression of being laid-back, relaxed and charming, but he had been like a different person that day. If it hadn't been for James's intervention she didn't know what might have happened.

She had kept Toby at arm's length ever since!

'The two of you were involved, but you claim on this occasion Toby tried to force you…?' Rufus repeated sceptically.

'We were not, nor have we ever been, involved!' she defended. 'If you must know, he terrified the life out of me that day.'

'Why do I have trouble believing you?' Rufus mocked.

Because he had never believed her, Gabriella knew. Not one single word she said. And he must have even more trouble believing this, when he knew how wildly she responded to him.

But that was Rufus, the man she loved, and Toby—she hated Toby!

'Your father put a stop to it and threw him out of the house,' she insisted defensively.

'And out of his will, it seems,' Rufus drawled. 'What were

you doing, Gabriella, crying wolf and so eliminating some of the competition? Perhaps I was going to be next?'

'You can't seriously believe that?' she gasped.

'Why not?' He shrugged. 'As it turned out, my father, obviously believing you to be a poor, unprotected female, misguidedly tied me to you, anyway. Perhaps you even suggested it to him, as retribution because I had always refused to fall for your—undoubted charms?'

She straightened defensively, stung by the fact that she had told him the truth and he refused to believe her. 'Not always!'

'No,' Rufus conceded dryly. 'As you say, not always. And, as it turns out, we do have great sex, don't we, Gabriella?' he snarled, daring her to deny her reaction to him.

As he couldn't deny his own reaction to her...

Damn it, he had never wanted a woman in the way he wanted Gabriella. Still. Even knowing what she was.

Gabriella swallowed hard, knowing it would be ridiculous of her to even try to deny her physical desire for Rufus. She also knew that it would be just as ridiculous for either of them to claim it would never happen again. Their response to each other was explosive, and just as unpredictable.

'Yes,' she acknowledged huskily.

He nodded. 'Maybe by the time I get back from New York I might feel like—exploring, that part of our marriage again!' he sneered. 'I would suggest you stay away from Toby while I'm away,' he said sharply.

As if that was going to be such a hardship!

If she ever spoke to Toby again it would be to tell him exactly what she thought of him and his lies.

'In the meantime, I really do have to get back to work now,' Rufus drawled. 'I have several things to arrange before I have to leave later this evening.'

Gabriella felt totally miserable at the two of them parting like this. It was obvious he didn't believe a word she had said about Toby. In fact telling him about that day three months ago just seemed to have made the situation worse, and reinforced his suspicions regarding his father's will and the reasons behind it being worded in the way that it was.

She had no idea when Rufus would be back from New York. A few days he had said he would be away, but what, exactly, did that mean? Two days? Three? Four? A whole week?

God, she hated herself for her own weakness in loving and wanting him in the way she did, when he so obviously didn't, and never would, feel that way about her!

'What do you want me to tell Holly?' she prompted as he would have left.

Rufus turned back. 'I don't want you to tell Holly anything,' he rasped. 'I have to go back to the house to pick up some of my things, and I'm more than capable of dealing with Holly myself,' he assured her with cold dismissal.

In other words, this was yet another part of his life that was none of her business!

CHAPTER SEVEN

GABRIELLA heard just how capable of dealing with Holly himself Rufus was when she returned to Gresham House late that afternoon!

'You promised me I could come with you the next time you went to New York!' Holly was accusing.

'Because I thought it would be next month when you're on half-term holiday!' Rufus came back impatiently, their voices loud enough to be heard as Gabriella walked past the family sitting-room.

'Then why can't you go next month?' Holly demanded angrily.

'Because I can't!' Rufus told her uncompromisingly.

Should she go in and break it up? Gabriella wondered. Or should she just leave them to it?

Considering she was probably the reason for Rufus's mood being so uncompromising in the first place, and Rufus would probably regret his attitude as soon as he left the house, perhaps it would be better if she *didn't* just leave them to it.

But Gabriella knew that if she interrupted them it was

more than likely she would become the focus of the resentment of both of them...

So what was new?

She pushed open the sitting-room door, and saw Rufus and Holly glaring at each other like adversaries across the room. They looked so much alike at that moment that Gabriella felt her heart tighten. Holly was very tall for her age, and as well as having that dark blonde hair and glittering green eyes her creamy cheeks were red with the temper that Rufus, as an adult, had learnt to control.

At least, usually...

As Gabriella had expected, they both turned their glaring green gazes on her. 'Anything I can do to help?' she enquired lightly.

'No!' Holly told her rebelliously.

'Don't be rude to Gabriella, Holly,' Rufus admonished abruptly.

'Why not? You are!' Holly came back defiantly.

Gabriella raised dark, mocking brows as Rufus gave a pained wince at the criticism.

Rufus frowned darkly, not aware that he had ever been rude to Gabriella in front of Holly. Although perhaps the fact that he had chosen to stay out of the house all weekend rather than be with his new wife was enough to show Holly the reluctance he had to spend time with Gabriella?

Which wasn't reluctance at all, just an effort to avoid this deepening physical need he had of her!

His mouth firmed. 'What Gabriella and I choose to do as adults is none of your concern, Holly.'

'You're breaking your promise about taking me to New York!' Holly tearfully returned to the subject of their argument.

'I am not,' Rufus defended frustratedly.

He had been having this same argument with Holly for the last ten minutes—and was getting precisely nowhere. Women, even seven-year-old ones, he had decided, could be extremely unreasonable!

'I'm sure there's a very good reason why Daddy can't take you with him this time, Holly,' Gabriella put in huskily.

Rufus looked at her warily. After the way the two of them had parted earlier this afternoon, her defence of his actions where his daughter was concerned came as something of a surprise.

'At least he isn't taking you, either!' Holly scorned.

'Holly—'

'You're right, he isn't,' Gabriella came back easily. 'Which means that you and I could spend the next few days getting to know each other better.'

'I don't want to know you better,' Holly told her defiantly.

'Holly, you will apologize at once!' Rufus snapped.

'I won't,' his daughter came back rebelliously.

'You damn well will,' he assured her firmly.

Holly shot Gabriella a resentful glare, obviously knowing by her father's anger that she had gone too far. 'I'm sorry,' she muttered insincerely. 'But she can't tell me what I can or can't do—'

'Holly, that is enough!' Rufus had come to the end of his patience, probably not before time if Gabriella's disapproving expression was anything to go by.

But Holly had always been his Achilles heel. Rufus was very aware of the fact that her mother had left her when she was only a baby, and so he tried to compensate for that. Overcompensate, probably. Because, as she got older, his daughter had come to realize that she was his weakness, too...

'Gabriella is trying to be kind to you.' Although God knew why based on this exhibition! 'Not that you deserve it when you're behaving like this,' he added disgustedly. 'How about I bring you a present when I come back from New York?' he prompted as Holly still pouted disappointedly.

'What sort of present?' Holly prompted suspiciously. 'The only thing I want is a pony, you know that.'

'I hardly think Daddy can bring you a pony back from New York,' Gabriella was the one to answer her reasonably. 'Isn't the fact that Daddy brings himself back better than a present?'

Holly looked at Gabriella uncertainly now. 'Well...yes. But—'

'There you are, Rufus.' Gabriella gave him a bright smile. 'Holly can do without a present this time.'

'I didn't say that!' Holly protested indignantly.

'I'm sure Daddy is going to be far too busy this trip to go present-hunting. Aren't you, Rufus?' Gabriella prompted firmly.

Rufus wasn't sure he knew what the conversation was about any more. Except that Gabriella obviously didn't approve of his bringing Holly a present back from New York as a way of settling the argument.

Certainly Holly's behaviour so far hadn't been exactly amenable, but he had never been on a business trip and not brought Holly a present back. And while he was reluctantly grateful to Gabriella for diffusing the argument somewhat, her interference was bordering on telling him what to do now.

And he didn't like it any more than Holly did!

'I believe you just have time to go upstairs and wash before tea, Holly,' Gabriella added purposefully.

Holly shot her another uncertain look, obviously not quite sure, after her father's rebuke, what to do next.

Which was Gabriella's intention. Holly was a lovely little girl to look at, beautiful in fact, but something that had also become blazingly obvious to Gabriella in the last few minutes was that she was also a very spoilt one!

Not Holly's fault, of course. And probably not completely Rufus's, either. After all, he had been doing his best to bring Holly up on his own for the last seven years, which wasn't an easy task for a man alone. Especially when it must have been easier to shower Holly with presents over the years in order to keep the peace.

But her own mother, Gabriella knew, would never have put up with such behaviour from her, and she didn't think Rufus should accept it from Holly, either. No matter how much he loved his daughter.

For a man who was so strong-minded and opinionated in other parts of his life—mainly her!—Rufus certainly seemed to have a blind spot where the upbringing of his daughter was concerned.

'I think you probably owe Daddy an apology before you go, too,' she added softly.

Holly looked even more perplexed, obviously never having

been reprimanded in this way before, glancing at her father now as if for guidance.

Rufus had no idea what to do about this situation, and in fact he could quite well have done without it.

At the moment he was still furious with Gabriella because of her meeting with Toby; he still had no idea whether it had been arranged or was accidental. Or whether to believe what she had told him happened with Toby three months ago. She seemed genuinely upset about the incident, and her disgust towards Toby had seemed genuine, too, but—

He just didn't have the time before he went to New York to find out whether or not she was telling him the truth!

And now this problem with Holly had blown up completely out of the blue.

He had to go to New York, and that was all there was to it, and it wasn't a situation he wanted to take Holly into.

But, if he was honest with himself, he knew it was this deepening desire he had for Gabriella, and all the uncertainties between them, that made leaving more difficult for him than it had ever been before. In fact, half of him wanted to say to hell with it and take her with him. He didn't even have to tell her why; he could easily have used keeping her as far away from Toby as possible as the reason for his demand.

But once in New York he had no doubts that he wouldn't let Gabriella out of bed for the first twenty-four hours. Which would totally defeat the object of his urgent need to be in New York in the first place.

No, much as he wanted to, he couldn't take Gabriella with him.

But neither could he understand her deliberate interference in his dilemma with Holly. The woman he thought she was would have enjoyed seeing this inability on his part to control his own daughter…

'Your father is still waiting, Holly?' Gabriella prompted again firmly.

Holly swallowed hard, shooting Gabriella another uncertain glance before turning to give him a rueful smile. 'I'm sorry if I was rude to you just now, Daddy,' she said huskily before turning to give Gabriella another rebellious glare. 'But just because Daddy is going to be away is no reason for you to think you can order me about and tell me what to do—'

'Oh, but she can, Holly,' Rufus assured her sternly.

Holly frowned at him. 'But—'

'If Gabriella tells you to do something while I'm away, I shall expect you to do it,' he told her firmly.

'She isn't really my mother—'

'No, but she is an adult living in this house,' he insisted decisively. 'And as such, you will treat her with the respect she deserves.'

Gabriella watched as Holly obviously fought an inner battle with herself for several seconds, not knowing whether to carry on arguing or—

She turned on her heel and ran out of the room!

And Gabriella very much doubted it was to go and wash her hands before tea!

'Thank you,' she told Rufus huskily.

He frowned his confusion, his face slightly pale from this altercation with his young daughter. 'For what?'

'For backing up my authority in front of Holly.' She shrugged. 'Knowing how you feel about me, I'm sure you didn't particularly want to, but I would have lost Holly completely if you had sided with her.'

Holly, like her mother before her, had a habit of either crying or throwing temper tantrums when she couldn't get her own way. His fault, probably, Rufus accepted impatiently. But Holly was only a child, and over the years it had perhaps become too easy to be indulgent to his motherless daughter.

He looked guardedly at Gabriella, still surprised she had taken an interest in Holly in the first place. 'And how do I feel about you?' he prompted bitterly.

She grimaced. 'Perhaps it would be better if we just avoided that subject for now.'

'Perhaps,' he conceded, studying her through narrowed lids. 'But I take it from your earlier comments that you think I spoil Holly?'

She gave a shrug. 'She's only seven now, Rufus, but if you carry on like this she will be a monster by the time she's seventeen!'

His mouth twisted derisively. 'And you would know all about that, wouldn't you?'

Gabriella stiffened. No conversation between them, it seemed, even one about his over-indulged daughter, could pass without Rufus taking a pot-shot at her.

She met his gaze unblinkingly. 'According to your theory the reason I was a mercenary little gold-digger at seventeen was because I hadn't been spoilt enough as a child!'

'I don't believe I ever specified it was only at the age of

seventeen!' he rasped harshly. 'Where did you disappear to again this afternoon?'

The question came completely out of the blue, throwing Gabriella slightly off guard, the colour heating her cheeks as Rufus looked at her with narrow-eyed appraisal.

'How do you know I disappeared at all?' she prompted slowly.

'You're working in Gresham's now, Gabriella—there isn't much goes on there that I don't know about!' he assured her grimly.

'Why do you want to know?' she evaded, knowing that Rufus probably thought she had met up with Toby again, but at the same time having no intention of telling him where she had really been. That was her business for now. Rufus would get to hear about it all in good time. Her time.

His mouth thinned. 'Don't try and play games with me, Gabriella. No matter what Toby may have said this afternoon, you won't win anything with me,' he assured dismissively.

She sighed. 'It isn't a contest, Rufus—'

'You're right—it isn't!' he rasped with certainty. 'Set yourself up with Toby against me and I'll tie you up in the courts so long you'll be eighty before either of you inherits anything!'

She breathed in deeply. 'I've already told you how I feel towards Toby, and the reason why I feel that way.'

Yes, she had, Rufus acknowledged impatiently. And if what Gabriella had told him was what really happened, then his father shouldn't have just thrown Toby out of the house three months ago, and changed his will, he should have had Toby charged with attempted rape!

If what Gabriella said was true…

He breathed deeply. 'Maybe when I get back from New York I should go and have a little chat with Toby…?'

'Go ahead,' she invited, her gaze unwavering from his.

There was something different about Gabriella this afternoon, he realized as he studied her through narrowed lids. She wasn't quite as defensive as she had been—in fact she wasn't responding to his taunts in the normal way at all…

'Why do you have to go to New York so urgently?' she prompted interestedly now.

Just like any other wife when her husband came home and told her he had to go away urgently on business…!

'Why the interest, Gabriella?' he questioned.

She shrugged. 'I just wondered what was so—urgent, you can't take Holly with you.'

She hadn't wondered any such thing, Rufus realized incredulously. Gabriella thought he was going to New York to be with another woman, and that Holly would just be in the way of that relationship!

As if he could possibly be interested in any other woman when Gabriella herself had him so tied up in knots he couldn't think straight most of the time.

His mouth twisted mockingly. 'You could always come with me, Gabriella,' he invited derisively—and totally in contradiction of the decision he had made minutes earlier. 'Although I couldn't guarantee you would see much of New York!' he added, watching intently to see her reaction.

His eyes, Gabriella realized, were now gleaming with a far different emotion from anger.

Rufus still wanted her…

How he could feel that way, believing what he did about her, she had no idea. But she knew by that gleam in his eyes, the slight flush to his cheeks, that Rufus desired her.

She met his gaze unblinkingly. 'I've seen New York,' she said. 'I went there with my mother and James a couple of years ago Christmas shopping.'

'So you did,' he drawled. 'Do I take it from that you want to come with me?'

Did she?

Oh, yes!

She hated the thought of him going away now, with things so unsettled between them. But at the same time she knew he was still angry at what he considered her duplicity with Toby, and that if she went with him to New York he would probably make her pay for that anger.

She shook her head slowly. 'I don't think that would be a good idea when you've already told Holly she can't go. She dislikes me enough as it is,' she added ruefully.

'She doesn't know you well enough to dislike you—'

'That's never seemed to stop you!' she pointed out dryly.

His mouth thinned. 'We both know exactly why I distrusted you from the beginning, Gabriella—'

'Even if what you believed about my mother had been true—which it wasn't,' she snapped defensively before he could speak, 'that was still no reason for you to decide I'm a manipulative little gold-digger!'

Rufus eyed her mockingly. 'And your behaviour in Majorca? You deliberately set out to seduce me that day, Gabriella. Am I to believe that was just—youthful curiosity?'

Because he was never going to believe she had been in love with him!

'It was!' she claimed heatedly. 'You were my good-looking stepbrother, obviously experienced, and I was—at the time I was infatuated with you!' she admitted breathlessly.

Rufus gave a humourless smile. 'And I suppose I crushed all your girlhood dreams?' he taunted.

Yes, he had.

Just as he was crushing the wholly adult love she had for him now.

She shook her head. 'You wouldn't care if you had,' she acknowledged quietly.

Rufus looked at her bowed head, at those long lashes sweeping her creamy cheeks, and resented the feelings of guilt she aroused in him even as he dismissed them as unnecessary. Gabriella had known exactly what she was doing five years ago. She had been dressed—or in this case, undressed!—for the part.

'You're right, I wouldn't care,' he confirmed harshly, his hands clenched at his sides as he desperately tried to resist the temptation he had to take her in his arms and make love to her, to give himself one more memory of her to take with him to New York. It was a fight he lost...

Gabriella looked up, her eyes wide as Rufus took her in his arms to crush his mouth down on hers in a kiss that demanded and took, his hands firm on her hips as he held her against his hardness, his hands moving to cup her bottom as he pressed her into him.

It was a kiss meant to punish, to claim possession, rather

than give pleasure. And in that it succeeded, as Gabriella knew that she wanted no other man but Rufus to touch and hold her like this, no matter how he felt towards her.

His eyes glittered as he wrenched his mouth away from hers and put her firmly away from him. 'Stay well away from Toby while I'm away,' he advised harshly.

Gabriella watched, tears gleaming in her eyes as Rufus strode forcefully from the room without so much as a second glance.

Because she meant nothing to him.

Because he felt nothing but desire for her.

A desire he satisfied whenever, and wherever, he felt like it.

A desire she had no weapons against.

Just as she had learnt today that she had no defences against the love she felt for him.

Which was why, this afternoon she had visited David Brewster to start the legal process that would ensure one day Rufus would have no choice but to believe her.

It might turn out to make absolutely no difference to Rufus whatsoever, but at least she would know, when in six months' time she gave him back the twenty-five million pounds he claimed were all she was interested in, that she had proved him completely wrong about her.

Her life, without Rufus in it, would be empty, but at least he would know the truth.

CHAPTER EIGHT

GABRIELLA was having the most wonderful dream. In her dream Rufus was in bed beside her, holding her, making love to her, kissing her even as he explored every inch of her body.

Gently.

Tenderly.

Adoringly.

Which was when Gabriella realized she really had to be dreaming!

Rufus didn't adore her.

She quickly buried such thoughts deep in the back of her mind, desperately returning to that dream, to the Rufus who was serving her so erotically.

Because she wanted Rufus to adore her?

Oh, yes!

She cradled his head against her as his tongue moved lightly across her breast, her moan one of protest as he abandoned his caress.

But as the heat of his lips claimed its twin, and gently drew the aroused nipple inside the moist warmth of his mouth, her groan turned to a moan of pure pleasure.

'Do you like that, Gabriella?' he prompted huskily.

'Oh, yes,' she sighed achingly. 'Don't stop, Rufus. Please don't stop!'

'Tell me what else you like,' he encouraged throatily as his hand moved gently down the curve of her body, his fingers trailing a path of fire.

This was a dream, she told herself, and in her dream she could ask Rufus to do whatever she liked.

'I like it when you touch me here.' She moved his hand to cup the warm triangle between her legs.

'Like this?' he asked as he started to stroke her.

'Oh, yes,' she sighed achingly, the pleasure building deep inside her. 'Rufus—' She broke off with a breathless gasp as he moved until his lips touched her, his tongue hot and moist against her arousal. 'Oh, God, Rufus…!' she groaned weakly, totally lost as the pleasure surged hotly through her whole body, arching her back, her head thrown back as that convulsive pleasure soared to every part of her body for what seemed an eternity.

'Mmm.' She breathed her satisfaction, reaching down to pull him up to her, her mouth ready for his as he kissed her with a demand that told her this dream wasn't about to end just yet.

She smiled as Rufus broke the kiss to move his tongue across the sensitivity of her lips, tasting, licking, teeth gently biting as he once more trailed a path to the swollen thrust of her breasts, her hands entangled in the thickness of his hair as she arched against him.

'More?' he prompted gruffly.

'Oh, much more!' She gave a husky laugh of triumph as

she reached down to touch the rigid hardness of his body. Rufus was the one to groan with pleasure this time as he fell back against the pillows beside her.

Her hair trailed across his chest as she moved down his body, stopping along the way to plunder the hard tips on his chest, her tongue dipping into his navel, so close, but still not quite touching his arousal, the darkness in her dream giving her a boldness she had never known before.

'What do you like, Rufus?' she encouraged huskily. 'Do you like this?' Her hand ran the length of him. 'And this?' Her tongue moved along that same silky hardness. 'And this?' as her tongue encircled the tip.

'All of it, Gabriella! I like all of it!' he groaned, reaching up to tangle his hand in her hair. 'For God's sake, don't stop!'

She had no intention of doing so this time, kneeling between his legs, her hand encircling him as her lips captured him, feeling the strength of him beneath her as he shuddered at her touch.

'No more, Gabriella!' he breathed weakly. 'I want to be inside you.'

'But what do I want, Rufus?' She straightened on her knees, changing her position so that she straddled him. She moved temptingly along the length of his hard arousal, but refused him entry to her heated centre. 'I want you to beg, Rufus. Beg me to take you!'

She murmured her approval as Rufus pulled her towards him slightly, capturing her breasts with his hands, his thumbs moving rhythmically against the swollen tips, his hips straining against her as he begged softly for the release she could give him.

'Not yet, Rufus!' she groaned. 'Oh, not yet…!' she cried as she could feel her own pleasure peaking once more.

Gabriella arched against him as he took one nipple into his mouth, full and open to his touch as the pleasure surged low in her body and spread wildly to every sensitized inch of her as she thrust against him.

She collapsed weakly onto his chest, breathing deeply.

'Now, Gabriella?' he pressed urgently as he moved so that he was poised between her legs, his arousal pulsing against her.

'Please…!' she groaned, reaching for him, guiding him into her.

'I can't hold back any longer, Gabriella,' he warned gratingly. 'I need you too much!'

'Come inside me, Rufus,' she invited achingly. 'Now!'

She met thrust with thrust, her nails scraping across the broad width of his back as she felt them reaching a climax that was deeper and stronger than anything she had ever known, before curling against him in the sleepy aftermath.

Wow! was Gabriella's first thought as she woke to the sun shining through her bedroom window, stretching like a cat as she remembered the eroticism of her dream in every detail, a smile curving her lips as she recalled how she and Rufus had given to each other, taken each other, and then given again.

It wasn't the first dream she'd had about Rufus, but never in the past had they ever been so erotic, or so lucidly clear to her when she'd woken up. She felt as though she were still able to feel the touch of his skin, the warmth of his breath, the caress of his lips and hands, the bite of his teeth against her shoulder as he shuddered to climax—

There were teeth marks on her left shoulder!

But it had been a dream. Hadn't it…?

Her eyes widened in alarm, throwing back the covers to look down at her body. Her naked body. When the night before she had gone to bed in a cream silk nightgown. A nightgown that now lay on the floor beside the bed.

Oh, God, it hadn't been a dream.

Rufus had really been here in bed with her last night!

Her face paled as she remembered all that had taken place, her lack of restraint in demanding what she wanted from him, her boldness as she'd touched and caressed him in return.

But Rufus was still in New York, she reasoned dazedly. He had been in New York for the last eight days. He couldn't have been here with her last night!

But she wasn't imagining the slight redness to the curve of her breasts, as if from the rasp of a late-night beard against the tender skin. And she wasn't imagining those teeth marks on her shoulder, either!

No matter how she might try to reason this out, Rufus really had been here in bed with her last night, and none of it had been a dream at all!

No, Rufus couldn't have been here, she told herself again. He hadn't so much as spoken to her on the telephone the last eight days, but he had spoken to Holly, and Gabriella was sure he would have told his daughter if he had expected to return last night.

There was no if about it; Rufus *had* returned last night.

And how was she supposed to face him again this morning after the wanton way she had behaved?

But only in her dream, she defended with a rising indignation. To her it had all been a dream.

What—?

'It's almost eight-thirty, Gabriella, if you intend going to Gresham's today?' enquired a mockingly familiar voice.

Rufus's mouth curved at the self-conscious way she pulled the covers back over her nakedness, her violet eyes blazing with anger as she glared at him over the top of them, her hair a wild tangle of ebony.

He had been tired, weary, and emotionally drained from his unhappy trip when he had returned last night, sorely in need of the warmth of just lying beside a woman in bed in order to drive the demons away.

What had followed had been totally unexpected. Pleasurably so. But still unexpected. All the more so because he knew the two of them had been angry with each other when they had parted eight days ago. But last night Gabriella had given to him in a way that made his body grow hard again now just looking at her.

Gabriella frowned at him. 'When did you get back?' she demanded rudely, a part of her still hoping that she was mistaken, that their lovemaking really had been a dream.

Futile, she knew, but she could hope, couldn't she?

Rufus shrugged. 'About one o'clock this morning.'

Gabriella closed her eyes, praying to whatever god might be listening, before opening her eyes again to glare at him accusingly. 'You came to my bed last night!'

'I did.' He nodded, gaze considering. 'We are married, Gabriella.' He shrugged.

'Yes, but—but—I was asleep. Didn't know what I was doing. You took advantage of me!' she accused heatedly.

He strolled further into the bedroom, dressed casually in a deep blue tee shirt and faded denims. 'As I recall, you were the one who demanded that I be the one to beg…?'

Oh, God, she had, too!

And Rufus had begged, as she remembered, had pleaded with her to give him release…

She swallowed hard. 'I thought you were a dream.'

He smiled slightly. 'Have a lot of dreams about me, do you?'

Never like that one. And never so lucid, either.

Because it hadn't been a dream!

'Usually they're nightmares,' she snapped, wishing he would go away so that she might at least try to regain some semblance of dignity.

Although that was going to be extremely difficult to do in the circumstances.

Rufus's smile deepened. 'You can have as many nightmares like that one as you please! I'm more than happy to oblige.'

She would just bet he was!

'Will you just go away, Rufus?' she muttered impatiently. 'Haven't you humiliated me enough for one day?'

His smile faded, his gaze searching the paleness of her face, and what he saw there didn't please him one little bit.

Instead of leaving, as she asked, he moved across the room to sit on the side of the bed, reaching out to cup one side of her face as he looked down at her intently.

He shook his head. 'I'm not intending to humiliate you, Gabriella,' he assured her huskily. 'In fact, if anything, I should be thanking you—'

'Thanking me?' she repeated agitatedly, fingers tightly gripping the sheet as she still held it defensively up to her chin.

Rufus gave a weary sigh. 'I didn't tell you before—the reason I had to go to New York so urgently was because the manager there had been involved in a car accident.' He shook his head. 'He died five days ago. I—he was a friend, Gabriella. All the family are.'

Gabriella looked up at him searchingly, seeing the strain now in his face, the lines beside his eyes and mouth that hadn't been there eight days ago.

His expression was grim. 'The funeral was yesterday. I stayed around for as long as I could, but his widow's grief was just too— He had two young children, too, and they don't understand at all—I couldn't wait to get out of there, Gabriella,' he admitted shakily, his thumb caressing the pout of her bottom lip. 'I badly needed what you gave so willingly last night, Gabriella,' he added intensely. 'Can you understand that?'

His father, her beloved stepfather, had died only seven weeks ago, and Rufus's loss was obviously still as painful and raw as her own. It must have been awful for him to have to go through the trauma of yet another death, of a much younger man by the sound of it, and a friend.

'I'm so sorry,' she told him huskily. 'I had no idea.'

He hadn't felt he could talk to Gabriella on the telephone while he was away, Rufus acknowledged. His presence had been needed in New York, for the stunned staff at the

Gresham's there, and for Jen and her two children. If he had so much as heard Gabriella's voice over the telephone he wouldn't have wanted to stay in New York at all; he would have wanted to get on the next plane home.

He had got on the next plane home as soon as he had felt free to do so.

He had missed Gabriella, he realized heavily. Whatever the reason for this marriage, whatever her involvement with Toby—and he would find out exactly what that was now that he was back in England—he knew that Gabriella was fast becoming an essential part of his life. A part he wasn't sure he was going to be able to relinquish at the end of the six months...

He stood up abruptly, thrusting his hands into his denims pockets. 'Come down and have some breakfast with me,' he rasped shortly.

Gabriella blinked her surprise at his sudden shift of mood. For a few minutes, a few brief minutes, Rufus had actually shared some of his personal life, his feelings, with her. A lapse he obviously now regretted!

'Okay.' She nodded slowly. 'I'll come down as soon as I'm dressed,' she added pointedly as he made no effort to leave her bedroom.

'Oh. Right. I'll see you downstairs.' He nodded abruptly before turning on his heel and walking away, closing the door firmly behind him.

Gabriella collapsed back against the pillows to stare blindly up at the ceiling.

She had longed for Rufus to come back from New York, the eight days without him here seeming to drag interminably.

Although she had expected, once he did return, that they would continue to have the strained relationship that Toby had helped to maintain with his lies, with Rufus's distrust of her now overwhelming.

Rufus coming to her bed last night, needing her warmth and closeness, the two of them making love in a totally uninhibited way, showed her how wrong she had been about that. No matter how much Rufus distrusted her, the two of them could still communicate in a physical way.

She, because she loved him so deeply.

Rufus, because he still desired her no matter what else he might believe of her.

'Aren't you eating anything?' she prompted ten minutes later when she joined Rufus in the small dining-room, only a cup of coffee on the table in front of him.

He grimaced. 'My body clock is all shot to hell. Besides, I had coffee and toast with Holly before she went to school.'

Gabriella sat down at the table with her coffee and a croissant. 'I bet she was pleased to see you,' she said ruefully.

'If only to tell me what a bullying, unreasonable stepmother I've given her!' He nodded ruefully.

She raised wary eyes, reassured slightly by the fact that Rufus was smiling. 'Holly decided to eat in her bedroom for two days after you left.' She shrugged. 'When I heard about it I told her I had instructed the staff not to take any more meals up to her room, that if she wanted to eat in future she was to come down to the dining-room. It took a day of starvation for Holly to realize I meant what I said, but she came down for breakfast the following day.'

The battle of wills between herself and Holly hadn't been at all pleasant, and now, even a week later, Holly still barely spoke to her as they ate breakfast or dinner together; she merely ate her food and then left.

Rufus looked at Gabriella admiringly, still not sure why she had taken this interest in Holly, but grateful that she had. It was a strange feeling to have for a woman he had always avoided feeling any emotion towards—except undeniable desire.

'She wasn't too thrilled, going on your advice, that I hadn't brought her a present back, either.' He grimaced. 'She believes the two of us have "ganged up" on her, was the way she phrased it, I believe.'

The likelihood of that was so ridiculous that Gabriella couldn't help smiling. 'She obviously doesn't know our real relationship at all!'

Rufus studied her through narrowed lids. She looked beautiful this morning, her make-up only a foundation and blusher if he wasn't mistaken, her lashes naturally long and thick about her incredible violet-coloured eyes, her lips red and pouting—from his kisses the night before…?

'What would you say our relationship was, Gabriella?' he prompted huskily.

She seemed to think about that for a moment, slowly sipping her coffee. 'Armed, but total, physical awareness?' she finally suggested ruefully.

He laughed softly at the description. 'At times an uncomfortable feeling.' He nodded.

Gabriella looked at him searchingly. After their conversation before he'd left eight days ago, she had expected him to come back as insulting as when he went away. She certainly hadn't expected to be sitting here sharing breakfast with him after a night of lovemaking that still made her blush to think about it!

But there was a quietness about Rufus today, a questioning, as if the death of his manager in New York had made him question aspects of his own life.

Of course, she would be a fool to try to read anything into that where she was concerned, knowing the slightest thing could set his suspicions off again.

'So you decided not to bring Holly a present back after all…?' She decided to pursue what was a relatively safe subject.

He shrugged. 'Because of what happened, I wasn't in the mood to go shopping! Besides, Holly was very rude to you, and to me, before I went away. I thought about that a lot while I was in New York, and decided you were probably right; I have created a monster.'

A monster who could turn out exactly like her mother if he continued to spoil her in the way that he was, he had reluctantly realized, only interested in what she could take and not what she had to give in order to receive. He had disliked Angela intensely by the time they were divorced, but he knew it wasn't too late to correct the same faults he had unwittingly created in Holly at only seven.

He had also had a chance to observe Rob's two children after their father died, had seen the wholly caring way the ten- and twelve-year-old had tried to help their mother through all that by not burdening her with their own pain and anguish.

It had made him realize he would like Holly to become as selfless as they were. And that the example of that could only come from him.

And Gabriella, it seemed…

Making her more of an enigma to him than ever.

He really hadn't expected Gabriella to continue to take this interest in Holly while he was away, and even while he had listened to his young daughter's complaints about her this morning he had wondered at that interest.

There could be no possible motive, that he could see, other than a genuine desire to help Holly.

Gabriella didn't think of Holly as a monster at all, just a very over-indulged little girl who needed to be taught some manners.

'How are the alterations at the restaurant progressing?' Rufus asked.

Her face lit up. 'Very well. It's all been painted, in Mediterranean colours, golden creams and terracotta. The new paintings are up, real plants trailing down the walls, the kitchen has been refitted, I'm just waiting for the new chairs to arrive and it will all be finished.'

She was as animated as he had been when he'd opened the Gresham's in New York, Rufus saw admiringly, once again questioning the hard work she obviously hadn't minded putting into this venture. The even harder work to come once she had actually opened the restaurant to the public.

'Will you be ready to open on Monday as planned?' he prompted interestedly.

'Saturday,' she told him firmly. 'I want to try and draw in

as many Saturday shoppers as possible,' she explained. 'In the hope that they'll return early next week.'

A good marketing ploy, Rufus thought approvingly, the beginning of the week always much slower for customers than the weekend.

Reminding him that he had a business here in London himself that he had necessarily been neglecting for over a week.

He put his empty coffee-cup down on the table, picking up the pile of messages he had been glancing through when Gabriella had joined him. 'I have to go and make some calls this morning, and then go in to Gresham's this afternoon. Will you be in for dinner this evening?'

So polite, Gabriella frowned thoughtfully, not quite understanding this new, tentative relationship between them. Rufus's interest in the restaurant had been completely unexpected, as was his query about her plans for dinner this evening.

'Of course,' she answered warily. 'Where else would I be?' she added defensively.

He raised blond brows. 'I was only asking, Gabriella.'

'Why?' She still frowned.

Rufus gave a rueful smile. 'Because I'm interested to know whether or not I'm having dinner with my wife this evening.'

He hadn't so much as mentioned Toby since he got back, let alone asked her if she had seen the other man while he was away. Why hadn't he?

Probably because he had only thought she would lie to him if he did ask!

'Well, I shall be here,' she assured him dryly. 'Whether or not you will is another matter.'

His gaze narrowed. 'Meaning?'

She shrugged. 'Meaning you've been away for over a week. You must have—friends, who want to see you.'

Surprisingly the two of them had never discussed whether or not there were other relationships in their lives when they married. There was no one currently in her own life, but the existence of Rufus's apartment in town meant she couldn't be so sure about his circumstances.

She had had plenty of time to think of things like that with Rufus in New York, and had decided that there probably *was* a current woman in his life, and that she was far from the first woman to be held completely in thrall by him.

Rufus had no idea what was going on inside Gabriella's head. He couldn't read anything from her guarded violet eyes, but the meaning behind her words was pretty clear.

'No "friends" at the moment, Gabriella,' he assured her. 'My wife might not like it!' he added mockingly.

'And that would really bother you, I'm sure!' she came back scathingly.

She was trying to pick an argument with him again, he realized. And he wasn't in the mood to argue with her just now; he could remember their closeness last night too well, and had too many unanswered questions about her, to feel comfortable doing that.

Questions he needed answers to.

But not here. And not now.

Now he intended making his exit before she managed to embroil him in a fight he didn't want.

He stood up. 'I have to go and make these phone calls,'

he dismissed. 'We'll have time to talk this evening, if that's what you want.'

She didn't know what she wanted, she thought. She felt completely disorientated by this calm, almost pleasant Rufus.

Last night they had made love, wildly, explosively, and completely without inhibition.

This morning Rufus was actually talking to her as if her opinion interested him, as if what she had been doing while he was away interested him, too.

She didn't know him in this mood at all!

'Oh, by the way—' he stopped in the doorway '—I have a message here from David Brewster requesting that I call him when I return to England.' He held up the stack of telephone messages he had been reading earlier. 'Do you have any idea what he wants to talk to me about?'

Gabriella tensed in alarm. David Brewster had telephoned Rufus in the last eight days?

That meant he had phoned since she had returned to sign the agreement in which she gave everything back to Rufus, except the restaurant Gabriella's, at the end of these six months...?

'I have no idea,' she dismissed firmly, determining then and there that she had to get to a telephone and speak to David Brewster before Rufus did.

The contract had been drawn up in complete confidence, and was no one else's business but her own, but she knew David Brewster wasn't happy about it. He had tried to talk her out of making such a move, assuring her it wasn't what James had intended to happen at all.

Admittedly David Brewster wasn't actually her lawyer,

but in the strange circumstances of James's will, and the fact that David Brewster was already completely conversant with it, he had seemed the only logical choice for drawing up such an agreement.

But she had thought David Brewster understood it was a confidential agreement, and not for Rufus, as the recipient of that agreement, to know about until she chose to tell him.

So what other reason could there be for the lawyer to need to talk to Rufus?

CHAPTER NINE

'WHAT do you have there?' Rufus prompted inquisitively as he sat on the side of his daughter's bed, having come up to say goodnight to her.

Holly looked up from the book she was obviously deeply engrossed in. 'It's a book on horses. Gabriella bought it for me today as a present, she said because I was a very good girl while you were away. She said she thought I ought to read about caring for a pony before I ask you to buy me one,' she admitted awkwardly.

Rufus's eyes widened. 'She did?' he said slowly.

'Mmm.' His daughter nodded, obviously anxious to get back to her book. 'Gabriella said she used to have riding lessons when she lived here as a young girl, too, and that if I liked she would arrange some for me at the riding stable she used to go to.'

'She did?' Rufus puzzled, aware that he was repeating himself, but unable to do anything else in the circumstances.

The fact that Gabriella had taken the time to select a book for Holly on a subject that obviously interested his daughter was surprising enough, but that she had also suggested organizing riding lessons for Holly was even more so. It was certainly above and beyond what he could have expected from their bargain!

'Mmm,' his daughter repeated herself, too. 'Once she had talked to you about it, of course,' she added hastily. 'Can I have riding lessons, Daddy? Gabriella said she would try to arrange one for Sunday morning if you agreed.'

Gabriella did this... Gabriella said that...

This was quite a turnaround from the way Holly had felt about Gabriella nine days ago...

But maybe Holly was changing already. She certainly seemed to be. Which was all to the good.

But it was Gabriella's behaviour that puzzled him. Aware that he hadn't brought Holly a present back from New York, she had got his daughter a present instead, because she had been a 'good girl' while he was away. It was the way in which a present should be given, rather than as a sop to Holly's temper, as anything he had brought back for her would have looked.

Gabriella, it seemed, had more of an idea of how to bring up a growing little girl than he did...

'I don't see why not, poppet.' He leant forward to kiss his daughter on the forehead, knocked slightly off balance as she threw her arms impulsively around his neck and hugged him.

'Oh, thank you, Daddy! Thank you!' Her eyes glowed with pleasure as she lay back against the pillows. 'Gabriella said she would drive me to the riding stable on Sunday if you said yes.'

'That's very good of Gabriella.' He nodded. 'Perhaps I might come for a drive, too.'

'Would you?' Holly's face lit up excitedly.

Why not? He occasionally took Holly to the park, and sometimes the theatre if there was anything suitable on, but he couldn't remember the last time she had looked this excited about anything.

'I'll talk to Gabriella about it,' he promised, standing up. 'Don't read for too long,' he added affectionately as he moved towards the door.

Holly nodded. 'Gabriella said I should only look at my book until eight o'clock, otherwise I'll be too tired for school in the morning.'

Rufus was more perplexed than ever. 'She's quite right,' he agreed, slightly dazed.

'I—I think I was wrong to be mean to Gabriella, Daddy,' Holly said in a small voice. 'I—she's nice.'

Yes, she was, Rufus acknowledged with a frown. And maybe, just maybe, he had been wrong to be mean to Gabriella, too…?

It was time—past time—that the two of them talked!

'Can you tell her about the riding lessons when she comes back, Daddy?' Holly prompted anxiously.

'When she comes back?' Rufus repeated slowly.

Holly nodded. 'She went out just before you got home from work.'

Gabriella had gone out? But this morning she had told him she would be in for dinner…

'Did she say when she would be back?' he prompted lightly.

Holly shook her head. 'Just later.'

'Did she say where she was going?' Rufus was slightly impatient now, as he had expected to see Gabriella for dinner. He had been looking forward to having dinner with her this evening!

'Just out.' His daughter shrugged.

'Okay, poppet.' He nodded. 'See you in the morning.'

'I love you, Daddy.' She smiled.

'I love you, too, Holly,' he assured her sincerely.

He had never doubted his love for his daughter, it was his feelings for Gabriella that were such a mystery.

As Gabriella herself was turning out to be…

'Where have you been?'

Gabriella stiffened at the sound of Rufus's voice, turning where she stood halfway up the stairs, to find Rufus had come out into the hallway and was looking up at her.

It was after eleven o'clock, and she had thought—hoped—that everyone else—especially Rufus!—would be in bed by now. In fact the silence as she had let herself into the house had convinced her that they were.

No such luck!

Rufus looked dark and forbidding in the low glow given off by the lamp left on in the spacious hallway, his face all hollows and shadows, his hair shining like burnished gold as he looked up at her.

'I thought you said this morning you would be in for dinner this evening,' he reminded her abruptly.

'You haven't been waiting up for me, have you, Rufus?' she taunted.

'Hardly,' he bit out tersely. 'I had some work to catch up on in the study, and just happened to hear you come in.'

'A change of plans.' She shrugged. 'I decided to meet some friends in town instead.'

In truth, the thought of sitting down to dinner with Rufus, after what she had learnt from her telephone call to David Brewster, had made her feel nauseous.

'Don't look so disapproving, Rufus.' She laughed mockingly at his dark expression. 'I do have friends, you know! And one of them wasn't Toby, if that's what you think,' she added quickly.

His mouth twisted. 'I'm sure you have friends other than Toby. I didn't mean to imply that you hadn't.'

Gabriella gave him a sceptical glance. 'Yes, I do. And the friends I met this evening were all female,' she assured him defiantly. 'I can give you their telephone numbers if you want to call them and check!'

She was deliberately challenging him again tonight, Rufus recognized with a scowl. He wondered at the reason for it.

They had seemed almost like a normal married couple this morning as they had chatted easily over breakfast. And he could only approve the changes she had already made to Holly, the time and effort she had already expended on his daughter.

So why was she once again trying to create an argument between them?

'I don't want to check up on you, Gabriella,' he dismissed lightly. 'I was merely expressing my—disappointment, that you weren't home for dinner, after all.'

Gabriella eyed him scornfully. 'I'll bet!'

Why was she so defensive, for goodness' sake? Okay, so

she had changed her plans and gone out this evening instead of having dinner with him, but surely he should be the one that was annoyed about that, not her? After all, this was his first evening at home after being away for over a week.

And he was sounding more and more like a disgruntled lover than the husband that had been foisted on her, he recognized ruefully.

'Come down and have a nightcap with me, Gabriella,' he invited huskily.

Gabriella looked at him questioningly for several seconds, wondering at his motives for the invitation. They were hardly friends, so what possible reason could there be for them to have a cosy nightcap together?

Her brow cleared as the answer came to her. 'I'm not in the mood for sex this evening, Rufus,' she dismissed scathingly.

'Not in the mood for— Hell, Gabriella,' he rasped impatiently. 'Did I so much as mention anything about the two of us going to bed together?' He scowled darkly.

No, he hadn't. But she couldn't think of another reason why he would want to spend time with her at eleven o'clock at night.

She gave a humourless smile. 'We don't usually talk about it—we just do it!'

He winced slightly. 'You're still annoyed with me about last night. I thought I explained the reason I was in bed with you—'

'Why on earth should I be annoyed because you invaded my bed, my dreams, without invitation?' Her hand tensed on the stair-rail.

This wasn't going at all well, Rufus thought, frustrated. His offer of sharing a nightcap together had been just that, with no ulterior motive on his part.

Although he could see why Gabriella might think there was one…

So far in their relationship—Majorca excluded!—he had been the one to initiate all their lovemaking, Gabriella always responding—mind-blowingly so!—but never actually making the first move.

'How about we make a deal that the next time we make love it will be at your invitation?' he suggested wryly.

Her eyes widened before narrowing suspiciously. 'You would keep to an agreement like that?'

What the hell sort of man did she think he was?

A man who couldn't keep his hands off her for longer than a few hours at a time, that was what sort of man he was!

But that was because—

Because what?

He wasn't sure…

He had lived without love in his life for so long he wasn't sure he would recognize it any longer!

He did know he wanted Gabriella. All the time. He also knew that, for the most part, he enjoyed her feistiness. He enjoyed looking at her, too; she was one of the most beautiful women he had ever seen.

He also had every reason to distrust her.

But did he?

That was what he wasn't sure about any more…

And until he was, it might be better, for both of them, if

they didn't cloud the situation with this physical attraction that was so immediate every time they were together.

'Yes, I would keep to an agreement like that,' he agreed harshly. 'Now will you come down and have a nightcap with me?' he added impatiently, already starting to feel the pangs of self-denial. Just looking at Gabriella made him burn with wanting her, the denims she wore moulding to the tightness of her bottom, her breasts bare beneath a clinging black tee shirt.

Obviously if he was going to keep his word he had better get used to taking a lot of cold showers!

Should she go down and have a drink with him? Gabriella wondered. What would it really achieve, apart from increasing this ache she had to launch herself into his arms?

'Holly spoke to me earlier about your suggestion she take riding lessons,' Rufus told her softly.

Ah, he wanted to discuss his daughter. That was different.

'A small brandy might be nice.' She unclenched her fingers from the stair-rail, turning to walk down the five steps to the hallway.

She wasn't quite so sure once the two of them were ensconced in the cosy warmth of the small family sitting-room, having become even more aware of Rufus as he sat in the armchair opposite her. Aware of the strength of his arms under the white tee shirt, of his long legs encased in black denims stretched out in front of him as he relaxed back in the chair cradling his glass of brandy with his long, sensitive hands.

Hands that she loved to feel caressing her body as he drove her—

Great!

They had agreed that if there was to be any more physical contact between them, it would have to come from her, and within ten minutes of making that agreement she wanted him so badly she couldn't think straight!

She swirled the brandy round in her own glass before taking a swallow, filled with a different warmth now as the alcohol hit her empty stomach.

She had met up with a couple of girlfriends for wine and nibbles, but had eaten nothing else since breakfast this morning. Too much of this brandy and Rufus could be throwing her over his shoulder and carrying her up to bed after all—unconscious!

'You mentioned Holly's riding lessons…?' she prompted, carefully putting the glass of brandy down on the table, not intending to drink any more of it.

'Yes.' Rufus watched her through narrowed lids, his thoughts, as usual, unreadable. 'She said that you intend driving her to the riding stable where you used to go.'

'If you're agreeable, of course.' She nodded. 'I've never bothered to get a car, living in France and then London, but I do drive, and I'm sure there are several cars here that I could borrow for the morning.'

'I wasn't questioning how you were going to get her there, Gabriella,' he drawled ruefully.

'Then what were you questioning?' She frowned, the warmth of the brandy spreading through her whole body now.

Rufus shrugged. 'Whether or not you're sure you want to be bothered with actually taking her?'

She had finally felt as if she was making some progress with Holly earlier today, the little girl's pleasure in the book she had bought her completely unaffected, as had been her excitement when Gabriella had mentioned the riding lessons. But if Rufus would rather take her to riding lessons himself...

'Fine,' she snapped dismissively. 'I'll give you the telephone number of where I used to go if you want to take her there, but I'm sure there must be lots of other riding schools around here if you prefer to go somewhere else.'

Rufus gave a pained grimace, feeling slightly as if he were banging his head against a brick wall where she was concerned this evening. 'Gabriella, I wasn't suggesting that you didn't take Holly, only giving you a let-out if you would rather not.'

'And why wouldn't I want to take her when I've already offered to do so?' she challenged.

He gave a heavy sigh. 'Gabriella, what have I done that's put you so much on the defensive?'

Done?

What had he *done?*

He knew damn well what he had done!

Or perhaps he had thought that David Brewster wouldn't tell her about the divorce papers he'd had the lawyer draw up!

She had been able to hear the shock in David Brewster's voice when she'd telephoned him earlier today and asked him if he intended telling Rufus about the agreement *she'd* had drawn up, and he had assured her he had absolutely no intention of telling Rufus anything about it until the appropriate time.

But he had also told her why he had been trying to contact Rufus...

Normally, she was sure that the lawyer wouldn't have done, but as David Brewster had been dealing with both of them on this matter he'd had no reservations about telling her that their divorce papers were all ready for submission on the appropriate date.

As Mr Gresham had requested...

As Rufus had requested.

No doubt immediately after Rufus had walked in on Gabriella and Toby talking together.

Which meant he definitely hadn't believed a word she'd said.

Again.

And now he wondered what he had done to put her on the defensive!

So much for her realizing she was still in love with him!

Her eyes glittered with anger as she looked at him. 'I wasn't aware that I had ever stopped being on the defensive,' she scorned, standing up abruptly. 'Let me know what you decide to do about Holly's riding lessons.'

Rufus stood up restlessly, totally frustrated by this conversation. He had come back from New York, a slightly different man from when he had gone away, having witnessed Jen's love for Rob as she'd slowly watched his life ebb, and seeing her complete devastation when he had literally faded away. He knew it was going to take her months, if not years, to come to terms with what had happened.

In the same way his father had when Heather had died. In fact, his father's love for Heather had been so deep that he hadn't wanted to go on without her.

Rufus wished now that he had got to know Heather better,

wished that he hadn't allowed his cynicism and disillusionment after his disastrous marriage to Angela to colour that relationship.

As it had coloured his relationship with Gabriella.

Women were only after what they could get, he had decided after his divorce from Angela, and the fact that his father had given Heather thousands of pounds before they were even married had only seemed to confirm that belief.

But looking back he couldn't see how his father, a shrewd as well as intelligent man, could have been so deeply in love with a woman who was equally manipulative and conniving as Angela had proved herself to be. Which seemed to imply that Heather hadn't been like that at all, that there had been a perfectly legitimate reason for her needing that money.

A reason Gabriella flatly refused to share with him.

And who could blame her after the things he had said about her mother? About her, too.

Yes, he had changed, Rufus realized, and not just because he had witnessed Jen's loss. His burning need for Gabriella was also making him question opinions and decisions he had made based on his own cynical disillusionment.

Unfortunately, *he* had changed, but the damage and hurt he had caused, especially to Gabriella, were still very much to the forefront as far as she was concerned!

And so governed every word she said to him.

If he ever wanted things to be any different between them then it was up to him to try to change that.

'I've already decided what to do about Holly's riding

lessons,' he told Gabriella huskily. 'I would like you to take her. If you're sure you don't mind?'

Gabriella looked at him inquisitively, finding no answers in the hard resolve of his face. 'I wouldn't have offered if I did,' she dismissed.

He shrugged. 'It's a long-term commitment.'

'If she's still interested in six months' time, when this is all over, I'm sure you'll be able to drive Holly to her lessons,' she said dryly.

Once they had separated.

And she was safely out of both his and Holly's lives.

'You'll still be her aunt Gabriella even then,' Rufus pointed out.

She gave him a frowning glance, wondering why he even wanted to point out that tenuous connection.

'I think, Rufus,' she said slowly, 'that when the six months are up, it would be better, for everyone, if we never set eyes on each other again!'

Rufus drew in a sharp breath at the vehemence behind her words. She really couldn't wait to rid herself of this marriage, of him, could she?

But then why would he expect her to feel any differently? He had scorned, mocked, and taunted her from the moment they had first met, even more so since they had been forced into this marriage by his father. Just because Gabriella responded to him physically didn't mean she didn't hate him, too. In fact, she probably hated him all the more *because* she responded to him.

Once again, he knew it was he who had changed, but was still reaping the results of his previous actions.

He sighed. 'I'm sorry you feel that way…'

'I somehow doubt that!' Gabriella laughed humourlessly.

Rufus gave her a quizzical look, not wanting her to leave with this strain between them. 'Gabriella, I already knew you hadn't seen Toby this evening.'

She stiffened defensively. 'And how can you know that?'

He grimaced. 'Because when I tried to contact him earlier his flatmate informed me, ironically, that Toby's in America for a week auditioning for a film role.'

Her smile was just as humourless as her laugh had been seconds ago. 'Well, it's gratifying to know you realize I wasn't lying about that, at least!'

'Gabriella—'

'Why were you trying to contact him?' she prompted shrewdly. 'No, don't bother to answer that, I can easily guess.' She sighed wearily. 'I'm tired, Rufus, and I'm going to bed,' she added with finality.

Rufus let her go, knowing there was nothing more he could say tonight that was going to improve things between them, only make them worse.

If that were possible!

CHAPTER TEN

'I NEED to talk to you, Gabriella.'

Gabriella looked up from the book she had been reading, surprised to see that Rufus had quietly entered her bedroom without her even being aware of it.

An unusual occurrence, because these last two weeks she had always made sure she knew exactly where Rufus was when he was in the house—and made a point of avoiding going anywhere near.

Which was why, knowing Rufus was wandering about downstairs this evening, she had chosen to stay in her bedroom and read a book.

She looked at him coldly, determined not to be drawn by his arrogant good looks. Even if her heart had started racing just at the sight of him, with other parts of her body reacting just as warmly.

'What are you doing in my bedroom?' she demanded. 'I thought we had agreed that I would come to you in future, if at all. Which, you'll notice, I haven't done,' she added hardly.

Knowing how physical, how sensual, Rufus was, she had

been surprised—disappointedly so?—that he had kept to his promise. She had been so filled with burning frustration some nights as she'd climbed into bed, knowing he was only just down the hallway, that she had almost been tempted to go to him anyway, to take what she wanted, to lose herself in that heated passion that allowed her to think of nothing but Rufus, of his pleasuring her as she pleasured him.

But she hadn't. Knowing that Rufus intended divorcing her at the first opportunity was enough to quench those desires.

'I noticed,' Rufus drawled as he stepped fully into the room and closed the bedroom door behind him.

Signals of alarm swept through Gabriella, her breathing becoming slightly uneven, and her cheeks becoming flushed as her gaze followed his pantherlike walk across the carpet to where she sat. Her nipples tightened beneath the fitted white sports vest-top she wore, and the heat between her thighs made her shift uncomfortably.

God, she was hot and ready just looking at him!

If he should so much as touch her...

Rufus tried not to let his hunger for Gabriella show in his gaze as he looked down at her, drinking in her sensual beauty, the proud thrust of her breasts beneath her fitted top, the long length of her legs in trousers that fitted perfectly over her hips and thighs.

His hands clenched at his sides as he acknowledged his desire to rip the clothes from her body, to kiss every silken inch of her, to taste her naked breasts as he touched her and stroked her to shuddering climaxes that made her so wet and hungry for him.

As he was hungry for her.

But he had been wrong to assume that things couldn't get any worse between them. The last two weeks of barely talking and having Gabriella avoiding him whenever possible had been a nightmare. Gabriella walked out of a room if he went in it, rarely ate at home any more—rarely ate at all if her loss of weight was anything to go by—and spent the evenings when she wasn't out closeted in her bedroom, completely shut off from him and any attempt he might make to see or speak to her.

Like this evening.

And Rufus couldn't stand it any more. He wanted this woman until he ached with it. He couldn't eat, couldn't sleep, and the thought of one more night without her wild and wanton in his arms was unbearable. Unacceptable.

So he had come to her, knowing she had told him not to, but unable to stay away any longer. He wanted, needed, Gabriella, to the point where he would go insane if he didn't have her.

Rufus looked about as happy as she felt, Gabriella realized ruefully, the strain of living with her in the way they were obviously as awful for him as it was for her.

She forced herself to withstand the intensity of his gaze as he continued to look at her, knowing she had lost weight the last two weeks, her appearance not improved by it, either, her face too thin, some of her clothes starting to look loose on her. There really was such a thing as being too thin, she had realized.

'You're looking tired, Gabriella.' Rufus frowned. 'Is running the restaurant proving too much for you?'

Her face lit up at the mention of her pride and joy, pleased to be able to talk about such a neutral subject. Gabriella's had been an overnight success, some of her first customers having become regulars after less than two weeks of being open, and recommending the restaurant to their friends, too. It was what she had always hoped for, and failed to achieve so miserably the first time around.

'Not at all,' she assured him with some of her old energy. 'You should try it some time,' she added teasingly. 'Most of the other Gresham's staff have!'

'So I've heard.' He nodded, smiling slightly. 'The executive dining-room has been almost empty since you opened up. It was good of you to take some of the original staff back, too,' he added approvingly.

Once she'd learnt that Rufus had employed into other departments of Gresham's the four women who had previously worked in the cafeteria, she had been only too happy to offer them the chance of their old jobs back. Three of them had taken up the offer, while the other one was now enjoying working in the make-up department too much to want to leave.

But Rufus sounded surprised she had thought of those women at all.

'Why wouldn't I?' she said defensively, knowing Rufus believed she was so self-centred those women losing their jobs wouldn't even have occurred to her.

Rufus sighed, knowing she had misunderstood him once again. He never seemed to be able to say anything right where Gabriella was concerned.

'I was paying you a compliment, Gabriella, not criticising you,' he told her wearily.

She looked at him searchingly for several seconds. 'Oh,' she finally muttered awkwardly.

Rufus gave a rueful smile. 'Holly tells me she's enjoying her riding lessons.'

Holly had told him a lot more than that, but he was sure that Gabriella wouldn't want to hear how much Holly now approved of her stepmother, with the added comment to him that he should 'keep Aunt Gabriella as his wife'.

Considering he was fast coming to that conclusion himself, and Gabriella obviously could no longer bear to be anywhere near him, it wasn't what he had wanted to hear, either!

Gabriella, he knew, couldn't wait for this marriage to be over, couldn't wait to have him out of her life!

'She's doing very well.' Gabriella nodded in response to his comment. 'A natural, Gemma at the stables tells me.' She smiled.

Rufus nodded distractedly, searching for something else to talk to her about, not wanting to leave her yet. If he couldn't have anything else he could at least look at her.

'Toby is still in America—' He broke off abruptly, knowing that had definitely been the wrong thing to say as he saw the way Gabriella's smile faded and her gaze became wary once again. 'Forget I said that,' he rasped, giving a self-disgusted shake of his head. 'Damn it, I came in here because—because—'

'Yes, why did you come into my bedroom without being invited, Rufus?' Gabriella prompted hardly. 'Was it to insult me some more? To question whether or not I've heard from Toby? Which I haven't. And don't want to, either!' she added angrily, standing up. 'Or perhaps you want to insult my mother some more? That's usually good for a couple of minutes or so!' Her eyes glowed deeply purple in her anger. 'Come on, Rufus, I'm really interested to know what you're doing here!'

Rufus drew in a sharp breath, biting back the defensive reply he had been about to give her, knowing that he would achieve nothing by doing that except furthering his own misery.

He closed his eyes briefly before opening them again, forcing himself not to meet anger with anger. As he usually did. 'You really want to know what I'm doing here?' he breathed huskily.

'I'm agog with curiosity!' she came back sarcastically. 'I can hardly wait for the next instalment of your accusations!'

Rufus knew he deserved that. And more. But this ache, this burning he had for Gabriella, this need he had to be with her, was beyond his control. Hard enough to admit to himself, let alone Gabriella.

But unless he wanted to spent the next five months in purgatory, he was going to have to try.

'No accusations, Gabriella,' he told her with a sigh. 'Just an honest admission that wanting you, desiring you, and not being able to be anywhere near you, is driving me quietly out of my mind!'

Gabriella stared at him, too shocked to do anything else.

Rufus wanted her. Rufus desired her.

As she wanted him. As she desired him.

But she would never have admitted that to him. She would rather have stayed in her bedroom for the next five months than go to him and tell him that. And yet Rufus had just done so.

But was want and desire enough?

It was all Rufus was offering. And although she wanted more, the truth was, wanting and desiring him was driving her quietly insane, too.

'That's all, Gabriella.' He grimaced ruefully as he saw her expression. 'Just—come down for dinner sometimes, hmm? I'm not going to ask for anything more than that, only that you stop avoiding me in the way that you have been. That's not too much to ask, is it…?' He looked at her guardedly.

And he had every right to feel guarded after what he had just told her. Never, not in a million years, would she have ever thought Rufus would own up to wanting her in that way. Shown her, perhaps, by seducing her back into his bed—something she had been longing for him to do the last two weeks!—but never tell her in the way that he just had.

'Poetic justice, hmm?' He sighed as she made no reply. 'I'll leave you to get back to your book now.' He nodded abruptly before turning on his heel to move forcefully across the room, closing the bedroom door firmly behind him.

Leave her to get back to her book…? After telling her he wanted her?

He had to be joking!

How could she think of anything else, concentrate on anything else, after Rufus had told her that?

Instead she paced restlessly up and down her bedroom, fighting a battle within herself.

Nothing had changed with Rufus's admission. Nothing. He

still believed that both she and her mother had been gold-diggers, only after James's money, the pair of them. He still didn't believe her about Toby—although it was curious that he was still trying to contact his cousin. Lastly, significantly, he had asked David Brewster to prepare the papers in readiness for their divorce…

But that was because they would be separating in five months' time.

That had been the agreement when they had married, at the insistence of both of them, so why was she now so angry because Rufus had pre-planned that divorce?

Because it hurt, that was why. Because she was still in love with him. Because now that she had lived with him she couldn't even bear to think about after they separated, let alone arrange their divorce.

But this was here, and now, and shutting herself off from him in this way, refusing to admit her own physical need of him, was only making her miserable. And, if she understood him correctly, for the next five months Rufus was saying he could be hers whenever and wherever she wanted him. Instead of being miserable in her self-denial, she could enjoy all the heated passion that she knew Rufus gave her.

Five months to last her a lifetime.

She deserved that, didn't she?

What the hell was she dithering for? She was a twenty-three-year-old woman, well aware of her own wants and desires, no longer an infatuated eighteen-year-old schoolgirl, and Rufus was just down the hallway, waiting for the invitation she had stubbornly refused to give him the last two weeks.

She could hear the shower running in the adjoining bathroom as she let herself into Rufus's bedroom, throwing off her clothes as she crossed the room on bare feet, her vest-top beside the door, her sports bottoms near the bed, silky panties next to the bathroom door, quietly letting herself in, the sound of the running water blocking out the sound of her entrance.

She could see the outline of Rufus's body inside the wide shower unit, lean and muscled, the bronzed hair wet and slicked back as he held his face up to the battering of the power-shower.

The door slid soundlessly back as she stepped in beside him, looking at him, drinking in his male beauty, his body leaner than she remembered, but tanned and muscled, the width of his shoulders rippling powerfully.

Gabriella reached around him to pick up the tube of shower gel, squeezing some into the palms of her hands before putting it back on the narrow shelf, rubbing the gel to a soapy froth before beginning to massage it into his shoulders and back.

If Gabriella being here was just a figment of his imagination, if this was just a dream, then Rufus didn't want to wake up. Ever!

He kept his eyes closed as the warmth of the shower water continued to cascade down on them, lost in the magic as her hands ran the length of his spine to his buttocks, tensing slightly as she caressed there, before she moved down the long length of his legs, his arousal already full when she reached around for him.

'Turn around,' she invited huskily.

He did, his eyes still closed, groaning low in his throat when he recognized that it was no longer Gabriella's caressing hands he felt but the warmth of her lips and mouth as she took him inside her.

Dear God…!

He looked down at her then, at the wet tumble of her dark hair down the length of her spine, her eyes purple as she looked up at him, before she once again claimed him into the warmth of her mouth.

His hands became entangled in the dark thickness of her hair, holding her against him; he had never known pleasure like this before. It was spiralling, building, surging, and his fingers tightened in her hair to pull her back when he knew he was almost at the point of no return.

'Now you,' he breathed huskily, pulling her to her feet as he kissed first her eyes, then her cheek, her mouth, the long column of her throat and the swell of her breasts. Gabriella's groan of pleasure told him how much she liked him doing that.

She was slick and wet, her body willowy slender as Rufus moved to kneel before her, gently parting the dark curls to find the centre of her arousal. Gabriella trembled against him as his tongue caressed and stroked, and she moved her legs slightly apart to allow him inside her.

Her hands clung desperately to his shoulders as she began to convulse around his fingers, but Rufus continued to tease her with his tongue, prolonging her climax until she collapsed weakly against him.

Rufus stood up, needing to be inside her now, wanting all her heat around him, surrounding him, taking him to the point she'd just reached.

Gabriella's eyes widened as she felt Rufus lifting her, his

arms about her thighs as she wrapped her legs about his waist. His hands cradled her as the hardness of him slid slowly inside her and she closed about him, each thrust of his body causing a responding trembling of her silken sheath, the pleasure quickly building again as his thrusts became more powerful with the approach of his own release.

A release that took Gabriella with it, and she cried out Rufus's name as she shuddered to another climax, the tightening of her inner muscles seeming to make their pleasure last an eternity.

Rufus rested his forehead against hers, breathing deeply. 'You are an amazing woman, Gabriella Maria Lucia Gresham,' he told her achingly.

Gabriella gave a husky laugh of satisfaction. 'You're pretty incredible yourself, Rufus James Gresham.'

Rufus raised his head to look down at her, her eyes a glowing violet, cheeks flushed, her mouth swollen from his kisses. 'I'm not even going to ask what changed your mind.' He shook his head. 'Just thank my good luck that you did!'

She looked at him and smiled in relaxed satisfaction.

Rufus grinned back and then turned off the shower before carrying her back into the bedroom, smiling again as he saw the trail of her clothes across the room.

'We'll make the bed all wet,' she protested.

'You aren't supposed to be practical after what we've just done!' he admonished teasingly.

Practical was the last thing she felt! 'I was thinking of you.'

Rufus shook his head. 'I'm happy just being with you like this,' he assured her huskily.

He lay on the bed with her, with his head buried against Gabriella's creamy throat. Breathing deeply, he knew he had been taken beyond anything he had ever known before, with any woman, and still he wanted her, wanted more.

Soon, soon he would take her again.

And again.

And again.

He knew that he would never be able to get enough of Gabriella, and that wanting her, being part of her, was in his blood. And he knew that it always would be.

Just as Gabriella herself would always be a part of him…

Gabriella woke lethargic.

Satiated.

And alone.

The bed beside her was still warm from Rufus's presence, but he was no longer there.

Instead, there was just a white sheet of paper on the pillow that read, 'My darling Gabriella, I've gone to see Toby, Yours, Rufus'…

CHAPTER ELEVEN

'GABRIELLA! Why the hell haven't you taken any of my calls?'

Gabriella frowned across the kitchen of Gabriella's as Rufus stood in the doorway, his face looking strained, his blond hair tousled, the denims and black tee shirt he wore looking rumpled and travel-worn.

Apparently he had come straight here from seeing Toby in America.

'I must have telephoned you half a dozen times in the last twenty-four hours!' he rasped accusingly as he came forcefully into the kitchen and closed the door behind him.

He had telephoned exactly seven times, Gabriella knew, twice here yesterday afternoon, five times to Gresham House during yesterday evening. And she had refused to take any of them.

What was the point?

If Rufus could just leave her after the night they had spent together, to go and talk to Toby of all people, then they really had nothing left to say to each other.

She shrugged, not looking at him as she finished tidying the kitchen after the Friday lunchtime rush. 'I've been busy,' she dismissed, glad she had a break coming up, not at all as composed as she wanted to give Rufus the impression she was.

Because she must have spent most of the last twenty-four hours crying. She had cried all day yesterday after she'd woken to find him gone, cried herself to sleep last night, and again this morning as soon as she'd woken up. And it couldn't go on.

She couldn't go on.

She couldn't stay in this loveless marriage any longer. No matter what the cost.

'Gabriella, what's wrong with you?' Rufus prompted, concerned, as she swayed weakly, crossing the room to cup a hand beneath her chin to lift her face so that she had no choice but to look at him.

God, she loved this man.

Loved him to the point of distraction. Loved him so much that nothing else mattered but him.

And she had to leave him.

She met his searching gaze unblinkingly. 'I'm leaving you, Rufus,' she told him firmly. 'Not in five months' time. But now.'

'What—?' Rufus felt himself pale, shaking his head in denial. 'You can't mean that, Gabriella—'

'Oh but I do,' she said flatly.

'No,' he insisted fiercely, looking frustratedly at the incongruity of their surroundings. 'We have to get out of here, Gabriella! I need to talk to you, to explain—'

'It's too late for explanations, Rufus,' she interrupted softly. 'Don't you understand? I can't take this any more. And it's not because I intend going to Toby, either!' she added fiercely. 'I just—I can't live with you any more!'

Rufus swallowed hard, unable to deny the complete conviction in her voice. 'No, Gabriella, I can't let you do that!' He shook his head in disbelief.

She gave a humourless smile. 'You can't stop me, Rufus. I'm sorry, I really am, but I can't—' She halted as her voice broke. 'I can't live like this any more,' she added firmly, lashes down as she shielded her gaze from his.

Rufus looked at her intensely, at the dark circles beneath her eyes, the hollows in her cheeks, the way she couldn't even look at him any more, and he knew he had to do something, say something to stop this wonderful creature leaving him.

The only thing he could say...

'Gabriella, I love you,' he breathed huskily. 'I love you, Gabriella!' he repeated forcefully, holding the tops of her arms as he shook her slightly.

Her long dark lashes flew wide above her startled violet-coloured eyes, Gabriella looking at him uncertainly now, as if to see whether or not he spoke the truth.

And he deserved her suspicion, Rufus knew, he deserved every accusation she had ever thrown at him.

As she, he was absolutely sure, had deserved none of the accusations he had thrown at her...

'Let's get out of here,' he encouraged huskily. 'I'll talk, Gabriella, if you will please listen, and if—if you still want to leave me after that, I—I'll help you to go,' he promised gruffly, knowing it would kill him to do that, but also knowing he had no choice. He could no longer keep this beautiful woman against her will.

Gabriella looked at him warily, not understanding this at

all. Could Rufus, of all people, have just told her that he loved her? Without knowing the truth about her mother? Without knowing the truth about her? What had Toby told him to bring about this transformation, for goodness' sake?

She didn't know what to do. It hadn't been easy the last twenty-four hours, coming to the decision she had, but at the time it had seemed the only one she could make. Now, a tiny candle of hope starting to burn inside her, she wasn't so sure...

Rufus saw her indecision and pounced on it. 'Come with me so we can talk, so I can explain? Gabriella, please!' he pressed urgently as she still made no reply.

She gave a slight shake of her head. 'I have the restaurant—'

'Lunches are over; I already asked one of the waitresses outside. Surely they can cope without you now for a while?' he pushed anxiously.

He had never felt so helpless in his life as he felt now just trying to get Gabriella to at least agree to listen to what he had to say.

Whether it would mean anything to her was another matter...

But he had to try anyway!

'Okay,' she sighed impatiently. 'But—'

'No buts, Gabriella,' he insisted determinedly. 'Er—do you have any other clothes?' He hesitated as he seemed to notice she was still wearing the white cotton top and blue and white checked trousers she had worn to work in.

Gabriella couldn't help smiling at the slightly bemused expression on his face. 'Yes, I have other clothes,' she assured him. 'I hardly travel up on the train in these! I'll meet you in your office in ten minutes or so, if that's all right?'

'Ten minutes, ten hours, Gabriella, I would still be waiting,' he assured her firmly.

She gave him another searching glance. He had been different when he came back from New York two weeks ago, and he was even more so now. And he had said he loved her!

That was what hurried her through changing into her own black tee shirt and trousers, before she made her way up in the lift to Rufus's office on the sixth floor.

'Go right in, he's expecting you.' Stacy smiled as Gabriella entered the outer office.

Gabriella entered Rufus's office shyly, expecting to find Rufus behind the desk, but instead he came out of the adjoining bathroom, stripped to the waist as he dried himself after freshening up.

Her eyes widened as she took in the broad width of his tanned shoulders and tapered waist, the tarnished blond hair slightly damp, too.

'Don't worry, I'm going to put some clothes on.' He gave a rueful smile as he saw her wary gaze, taking a clean shirt from behind the door and slipping it on, buttoning it but not bothering to tuck it into his denims.

Gabriella hadn't exactly been worried, as she knew that the physical attraction they had for each other was too strong to bother her any more. At the same time she was sure that simply falling into each other's arms and making love wasn't going to help to sort this mess out—it hadn't in the past. In fact, it appeared to be what had happened in Majorca that had started all the misunderstandings between them!

Rufus felt as nervous as Gabriella looked, eyeing her ruefully. 'Do you want to sit down? Or—fine.' He nodded as she sat down on the sofa at the back of his office.

He had never felt so nervous in his life, as he knew that everything depended on this conversation with Gabriella, and that without her his life was going to be more empty than it had ever been. Barren.

'You said you were going to talk if I would listen,' she reminded him huskily.

Yes, he had, and no matter what it cost his natural reserve, his deep-felt self-preservation, he had to tell Gabriella exactly how he felt about her. And why. Otherwise he was going to lose her for good. And that was just unacceptable.

He went down on his knees beside her, not touching her, but able to feel the warmth of her, smell her perfume. Just breathe in being close to her again.

'Gabriella, I didn't leave you yesterday morning because I wanted to—'

'Why else would you have gone?' she interrupted scornfully, still able to feel that sense of desolation she had known at finding him gone when she'd woken up in his bed. 'Not another emergency, surely?' she derided.

'Of a kind.' He nodded, his expression grim, his eyes having gone hard. 'I lay awake just holding you after you fell asleep on Wednesday evening. Unable to sleep myself. Thinking. And thinking. Somewhere around three o'clock in the morning I knew I had to go and find Toby—'

'You told me that in your—note,' she reminded dryly.

He nodded. 'But not why, I realized once I was on the plane to Los Angeles, which was why I began telephoning you so frantically once I was free of the airport. Gabriella, I went to find Toby to tell him that if he ever came near you again I would beat him to a pulp!' Rufus bit out harshly. 'Needless to say—' his mouth twisted with distaste '—Toby has decided to stay on in America indefinitely! As for my "note", as you call it—'

'Just a minute,' Gabriella halted him, aware she wasn't exactly sitting and listening as Rufus had asked her to do, but having too many questions of her own now to remain silent. 'Why would you tell Toby that?'

Rufus stood up forcefully, his hands clenched into fists at his sides. 'Because the bastard tried to rape you four months ago!' He was breathing heavily in his agitation.

Gabriella's eyes widened. 'You believe me about that now?'

'Gabriella, I've held you, I've loved you, touched you in the most intimate way, all the time with you proclaiming you hate me, and yet you've never shrunk from me in revulsion in the way you do with Toby.' Rufus shook his head.

There was a very good reason for that, she thought. She happened to be deeply in love with Rufus...

Rufus scowled. 'I finally realized, on Wednesday night after you gave yourself to me so freely, that there was no other explanation than the one you had given me. And if I had known about it then I wouldn't have been as forbearing as my father, I can assure you,' he added grimly.

Gabriella swallowed hard, finding it difficult to take all of this in. 'I thought you went to see Toby because you didn't believe me—'

'You mentioned my note, Gabriella,' Rufus rasped. 'I wrote it to "My darling Gabriella",' he reminded her intensely. 'I signed it "Yours, Rufus"—because I am yours, Gabriella. For what it's worth,' he added. 'I'm all yours. I always will be,' he said gruffly.

'But you want a divorce.' She frowned her confusion.

'What?' Rufus queried disbelievingly.

She nodded. 'You had David Brewster draw up the papers while you were in New York; that's the reason he wanted you to contact him when you got back—'

'Just a minute.' Rufus stopped her, at last beginning to see a possible reason for the change in her that day. He had expected to have dinner with her and she had deliberately avoided doing so by going out with friends, avoiding him completely after that, until he had thought he was going insane with wanting her, with wanting just a word or a smile from her. 'I didn't have David Brewster draw up those papers—'

'Well, I certainly didn't!' she protested, the colour coming back into her cheeks in her agitation. 'Besides, I spoke to David Brewster, and he told me that Mr Gresham had asked him to draw up the divorce papers—'

'But did he say *which* Mr Gresham he was talking about?' Rufus cut in softly.

Gabriella frowned her puzzlement. 'I don't understand—'

'It was my father, Gabriella,' Rufus told her patiently. 'He was the one who asked David Brewster to have those papers drawn up. Don't ask me why, but he did. It certainly wasn't me.' He moved to clasp her hands in his. 'Gabriella, I don't want a divorce, not now, not in six months' time, not ever!'

She was totally confused now; she had no idea either why James should have asked David Brewster to do such a thing. But Rufus had to be telling her the truth about that, and she knew she only had to make a single telephone call in order to know if he was lying. Besides, why should he?

She looked up at Rufus guardedly now. 'What do *you* want, Rufus?' she asked huskily.

He drew in a ragged breath, his hands tightening about hers until he saw her wince slightly. But this was too important for him to make a mistake now!

'I want *you*, Gabriella,' he told her softly. 'Forget my father's will. Forget the past. Forget everything but now. I love and want you so much now that if you leave me I'm just going to keep pestering you and pestering you, spend all my days haunting Gabriella's, my nights haunting wherever you go to live, until eventually you'll feel so sorry for me you have to come back to me!'

Gabriella gave a choked laugh. 'I could never feel sorry for you, Rufus,' she assured him ruefully. 'You're far too big, and strong, and—and self-contained, for me to ever feel sorry for you!'

He gave a shake of his head. 'Without you I'm none of those things. And I haven't been self-contained, as you call it, for some time. Since the afternoon of our wedding, if you must know. God, Gabriella, that afternoon—!' He closed his eyes briefly as he recalled the living flame of her in his arms that afternoon. 'You completed me that afternoon, Gabriella.'

He gazed down at her intently. 'Filled me, engulfed me, made me absolutely yours.' He shook his head. 'I've been fighting for my emotional freedom ever since!'

'You filled and engulfed me, too, Rufus,' she told him huskily. 'But—' Gabriella moistened dry lips '—I was a virgin that day, Rufus. I—I left so suddenly because I didn't want you to know that,' she admitted ruefully. 'I couldn't bear your ridicule if you should realize that.'

Rufus closed his eyes, remembering Gabriella that afternoon, the way she had given herself to him so completely.

All these months—years—he had been mocking her, and he had been her first lover, after all. What a fool he was!

'You took me to the apartment where you take your mistresses!' she reminded him frowningly.

'No, I only let you go on thinking that.' He grimaced self-derisively. 'I really do only use that apartment if I'm delayed in town on business.'

Gabriella looked at him searchingly, seeing only truth and honesty in that candid green gaze. 'But you knew what I thought, and yet you let me go on thinking—'

'Gabriella, I never said that I ever *wanted* to fall in love with you,' he rebuked gently. 'Look at it from my point of view. Please! Angela, Holly's mother, married me for what she could get in a divorce settlement. I thought your mother had married my father for his money. I thought you set out to seduce me in Majorca for the same reason—'

'I was in love with you!' she cut in protestingly. 'I loved you so much I ached with wanting you to love me in return! I've always loved you, Rufus. Always...' she repeated softly.

'Oh, God…!' Rufus choked. Now that he loved her, and ached for her to love him in return, he could see what he must have done to her five years ago.

'I fell in love with you the moment I set eyes on you,' Gabriella continued huskily. 'I never set out to trap you that day; I only wanted you because I loved you, and wanted to be with you, wanted you to love me in the way I loved you.'

Rufus was white now, lines of strain beside his eyes and mouth. 'And instead I mocked and scorned you until you hated me,' he agonized achingly. 'You were amazing that day, Gabriella. More, so much more, than I had expected. I daren't make love to you, because I knew that I would be lost if I did. And so I set out to make you hate me, instead.'

'I think you succeeded for a while, too.' She nodded. 'It certainly stopped me ever wanting to love anyone else, let alone become involved in a physical relationship!'

'God, Gabriella, no wonder the thought of marrying me five years later filled you with such horror!' he muttered.

But it hadn't. Not really. Because underneath it all she had still been in love with him. As she was still.

'Rufus,' she began softly. 'I only said it was partly because of our time together in Majorca that I haven't been involved with anyone else,' she reminded lightly. 'Do you really love me not knowing why my mother needed that hundred thousand pounds? Knowing that I borrowed money from James, too? Thirty thousand pounds, as it happens. Do you love me not knowing the answer to those things?'

'I would love you, Gabriella, even if you really were the

money-grabber I've so often accused you of being—damn it, I did fall in love with you believing that!' he admitted ruefully.

He must have done, because she still hadn't told him about her mother, and why Heather had needed that money James had so willingly given her. Or why she herself had needed thirty thousand pounds a year ago. And he had believed her about Toby with no proof whatsoever except what she had told him, and what he had come to realize from loving her.

She nodded. 'Then I think you should know that I still love you. That I've always loved you and I always will. And that's the real reason why I could never become involved with anyone else this last five years,' she added with certainty, only just realizing that herself.

Rufus stared at her as if he couldn't believe what she was saying.

He continued to stare at her, until Gabriella couldn't stand it any more, and launched herself into his arms as she had so often longed to do.

'I love you, Rufus,' she choked. 'I love you!'

'But—but you said you were leaving me,' he finally managed to gasp, at the same time holding her so tightly against him she could barely breathe.

'Because I love you,' she insisted.

Rufus shook his head dazedly. 'That makes no damn sense to me whatsoever,' he mused incredulously. 'But as long as you love me, as long as you'll stay with me, I don't care if anything else ever makes sense again!'

Gabriella gave a choked laugh, that laugh fading as Rufus began to kiss her.

Heaven.

Being in Rufus's arms, feeling the unconditional love he felt for her, was absolute heaven.

'Marry me, Gabriella,' he urged as he lifted his mouth from hers to kiss the hollows of her cheeks, the dark shadows beneath her eyes.

'We're already married, silly.' She laughed softly as she nestled against his chest.

Rufus shook his head. 'I want to marry you properly, Gabriella. I want us to have a blessing in a church, to say our vows and mean them, to know that we're doing so because we love each other.'

She gazed up at him with her wonderful violet-coloured eyes. 'If that's really what you want.' She nodded.

'More than anything,' he assured her huskily, cradling each side of her face as he looked down at her intently. 'You are the most important thing in my life, Gabriella. Without you I'm only half—a quarter!—alive.' He gave a self-disgusted shake of his head. 'I don't know how I've lived the last five years without you. If it's any consolation, no other woman has ever meant anything to me. How the hell could they after that afternoon in Majorca?' He groaned.

'But—' she frowned '—you didn't—only I—'

'Yes—and you spoilt me for any other woman,' he assured her fiercely. 'And how I hated you for it!'

'I would never have guessed!' she teased, kissing the hard line of his jaw.

He gave a self-derisive smile at her teasing. 'You're pleased about that, aren't you?' he guessed ruefully.

'Absolutely,' she acknowledged unhesitantly. 'Why should I have been the only one to suffer?'

'Why, indeed?' he acknowledged dryly. 'Where would you like to go for our honeymoon?'

'Majorca?' she came back mischievously.

Rufus laughed at her intended irony. 'I may not let you out of the villa for a month!'

'I may not let *you* out of the villa for a month!' she assured him huskily.

Rufus laughed again. 'Sounds good to me!'

'And me.' She nodded before moving back slightly. 'But there are still some things I need to tell you, Rufus—'

'I don't need to know.' He gave a decisive shake of his head. 'Whatever was between my father and your mother was their business, not mine.' And it really wasn't, he finally acknowledged. His own marriage to Angela had been one thing, but his father's marriage to Heather had been something else. As Gabriella was something—someone—else.

Completely.

'I wasn't actually talking about that.' Gabriella gave a slight smile. 'Although you do need to know why my mother—'

'Why do I?' Rufus reasoned. 'Whatever Heather's reason, I'm sure it was a good one. My father couldn't have loved her in the way he did if she hadn't been the woman he thought she was,' he added with absolute conviction.

Gabriella looked up at him wonderingly. 'You really have changed, haven't you…?'

He nodded grimly. 'I watched Jen, the wife of my manager in New York, sit by his bedside until he died. And I knew then that I had let my own prejudices and disillusionment rob me of so many things in life. I wish now I had got to know your mother better. And there is no way, absolutely no way, I am ever going to let you go out of my life, Gabriella,' he assured her as his arms tightened about her. 'No separation. No divorce. Just fifty or sixty years of being married to you, of seeing you every day, of loving you every day—'

'Of having children together,' Gabriella put in softly.

His expression softened. 'Only if that's what you want, Gabriella.' The thought of this gloriously beautiful woman pregnant with his child was enough to stop his breath, but he only wanted that if she did. He only wanted whatever Gabriella wanted for the whole of their future life together.

She swallowed hard, her eyes dark as she looked up at him. 'I'm pregnant, Rufus,' she revealed huskily. 'That's why I was leaving you.'

He stared down at her in stupefied silence, definitely having stopped breathing. Gabriella was pregnant? But—

'About four weeks, I think.' She nodded as if in answer to his unasked question. 'It happened that afternoon at your apartment after we were married, probably,' she added ruefully.

She hadn't been able to believe it herself when, getting out of Rufus's bed yesterday morning, she had instantly swayed and sat down again, at the same time remembering a couple of other instances when she had felt slightly light-headed in the last two weeks, occasions she had just put down to the emotion of the situation she found herself in.

But sitting there yesterday morning, thinking of the weeks since she and Rufus were married, she had realized that she hadn't had a period since they were married, so her first stop on the way into Gresham's yesterday had been to a chemist, where she had bought a pregnancy-testing kit.

Positive.

Her emotions had been mixed. Joy, that she was expecting Rufus's baby. Fear, as she knew that he was likely to accuse her of becoming pregnant on purpose in order to trap him. Her only solution had seemed to be to leave him. Even if by doing so Rufus lost Gresham's.

Rufus moved his hand down to cradle her abdomen. His baby. Their baby. Gabriella's baby.

He could hardly believe it!

'Are you okay about that?' he prompted anxiously.

'Oh, very,' she assured him with certainty. 'It's more than I ever dreamt of, more than I ever hoped! Oh, yes, Rufus, I'm very happy about this baby!'

'Then so am I!' He held her tightly in his arms as he began to kiss her, knowing that she was his whole world, that he couldn't go on another day without her.

'How do you think Holly will feel about having a little brother or sister?' Gabriella prompted minutes later.

Rufus gave a rueful smile. 'My daughter has already informed me that if I don't keep you as her mother she is going to be most unhappy with me!'

Gabriella laughed. 'And we don't want that, do we?'

'It's your happiness that concerns me, Gabriella,' he assured her firmly. 'That consumes me. God, I have so many things to make up for that—' He broke off as Gabriella put silencing fingers on his lips.

'Let's forget the past, Rufus,' she urged, 'and move on. We love each other. We have Holly. We're going to have a baby of our own. Let's just concentrate on those things, hmm?'

She was very forgiving, this woman he loved—and Rufus intended making sure he never gave her reason for regretting her emotional generosity…!

'There are just a couple of things I need to tell you—'

'We're moving on, remember, Gabriella,' he chided lovingly.

She shook her head, knowing these things needed to be said before they could do that. 'I need to explain about my own loan from James. And—and my mother's—'

'I told you I don't need to know,' Rufus said firmly.

'But I need to tell you,' she insisted, telling him of her own problems a year ago, the reason James had lent her the money. 'But there is a legal contract to say I owe the money. A contract I insisted had to be drawn up,' she assured him. 'But a contract I couldn't allow Toby, of all people, to get his hands on,' she added frowningly.

'Even marrying me was preferable to that, hmm?' Rufus muttered self-disgustedly, knowing now exactly why Gabriella had married him.

'Yes,' she smiled ruefully. 'But David Brewster also has another contract in his possession,' she told him softly, her expression wary. 'An agreement I had him draw up after Toby came to Gabriella's that afternoon and you suspected us of some sort of collusion. The afternoon I disappeared and you wanted to know where I had been,' she reminded him as Rufus frowned.

'I have a feeling I'm not going to like this,' he said slowly.

Probably not, Gabriella acknowledged. But at the time it

had been something that had to be done. To be revealed to Rufus when she considered the time was right. And here, and now, was that time.

'I've signed everything but my lease for Gabriella's, and that contract saying I owe thirty thousand pounds to James, back to you at the end of our six months of marriage,' she explained huskily.

Rufus's expression darkened. 'I really am the bastard you've always thought me, aren't I?' he muttered disgustedly. 'Well, that agreement can be consigned to the bin, Gabriella. Burned,' he added with feeling. 'From now on, my darling, we're going to be partners in everything, including the Gresham money and properties!'

Gabriella gave him a dazzling smile. 'I love you, Rufus!'

'I love you, too. More than life itself,' he assured her forcefully.

She believed him, and could already visualize the next 'fifty or sixty years' of their marriage, of being with Rufus, of having a family together, and knew that it was going to be magical.

'There's just my mother's loan to explain—'

'But I told you, that was between my father and Heather, is none of my damn business,' Rufus dismissed self-disgustedly.

Gabriella kissed him lingeringly on the lips before continuing. 'Some of this I didn't know myself until you told me about the loan and I spoke to my mother,' she began huskily. 'I knew my parents weren't exactly happily married, that my father was often out of work, that he was always out in the evenings, but I had no idea of the extent of his—irresponsibility. When I was a child I only saw that he was fun. It was only as I got older that I heard the arguments, saw how worried my mother sometimes was, that there was no money for bills that needed to be paid, for essentials, sometimes even for food—'

'Gabriella, please don't go on!' Rufus groaned.

'It's all right, Rufus,' she assured him softly. 'I want to tell you. My mother did what she could to keep her worries from me, but the truth is my father was a compulsive gambler. And after he died, my mother learnt that, not only had he remort-gaged our home to supplement his addiction, begged, stolen or borrowed money that should have paid our bills—tricking her into signing loan agreements and running up debts that amounted to over a hundred thousand pounds!—but that she wasn't even his real wife. He already had a wife in Italy that he had left behind years ago, never bothering to divorce her, but marrying my mother anyway. Marrying her and having me.' Gabriella blinked back the tears. 'My name isn't even really Benito!' she revealed huskily.

'No—because it's Gresham!' Rufus told her fiercely, holding her tightly in his arms. 'Dear God, Gabriella, how stupid I've been!' he muttered disgustedly.

'You couldn't have known, Rufus.' Gabriella shook her head. 'I didn't know myself until my mother told me the truth. I—it's unbelievable, isn't it?'

'Forgettable. Totally, and utterly forgettable. Because it isn't important. Only you, and here and now, are important,' he insisted determinedly, looking down at her lovingly. 'Now can we move on?' he prompted teasingly.

'Oh, yes.' She sighed her willingness to do that. 'All I

want, all I've ever wanted, is to be with you, loving you, having you love me in return!'

'For the rest of our lives,' Rufus promised emotionally. 'We are going to be so happy together, Gabriella.'

EPILOGUE

'WHAT do you think it says?' Gabriella prompted eagerly as she looked down at the letter in her husband's hand.

'Let's open it and see,' Rufus murmured indulgently.

Six months of marriage, five of them absolutely blissful, had brought about changes in both of them, Gabriella noted with satisfaction.

They had had their blessing in church, with family and friends around them, and Holly as bridesmaid, which was something she had taken great pride in. And their blessing gift to Holly had been that pony she had wanted, and now treasured, so much.

Rufus assured Gabriella often that at six months pregnant she looked absolutely beautiful to him, and from loving Rufus, and being loved by him, she felt beautiful, too.

Rufus had changed the most, no longer in the least cynical, but a relaxed and loving husband and father. A very loving husband, Gabriella remembered, smiling her satisfaction as she thought of their time in bed together this morning.

Before they had had to go to their appointment with David Brewster…

The six months were over, and the lawyer had asked that they come in to his office and see him on that day.

He had handed them a letter, addressed to 'Gabriella and Rufus', with the apology, 'I know you asked initially if there was anything further in Mr Gresham's will that you needed to know about, but this letter wasn't actually in the will.' David Brewster smiled ruefully. 'And it was only to be given to the two of you if you had decided to remain married at the end of the six months. I take it that you have decided to do so…?' he prompted with an indulgent look at Gabriella's obvious pregnancy.

Rufus's hand had tightened on Gabriella's. 'She wouldn't even get as far as the door if she tried to escape me now!' he assured with some of his old arrogance.

'Lucky I don't want to, then, isn't it?' Gabriella came back teasingly.

'I'm really so very pleased for you both,' the lawyer told them warmly as he shook both their hands as they left. 'I'm sure this is exactly what Mr Gresham wished to happen.'

Rufus looked down at the unopened letter now as the two of them sat in his parked car outside David Brewster's office. 'Knowing my father, I think this is exactly what he wanted to happen, too.' He smiled affectionately.

'Open it,' Gabriella encouraged, leaning against Rufus's shoulder as he did so.

My dear Gabriella and Rufus,

As the two of you are reading this, I know that my congratulations are in order, that the two of you have decided to stay married, and that David has destroyed the divorce papers I asked him to prepare in case I had made a terrible mistake, after all.

Those papers, along with Gabriella's contract stating she owed James thirty thousand pounds, had been destroyed five months ago, consigned, as Rufus had said they would be, to the incinerator.

But the fact that you are reading this tells me that I didn't make a mistake at all, that the two of you have realized, as I did long ago, that you are absolutely perfect for each other. Please forgive an old man for his interference, but I do love both of you so, and only ever wanted your happiness.

Rufus, Gabriella is the child of my heart, and I sincerely hope she is now the love of your heart, that you will protect and love her all your long lives together.

Gabriella, Rufus is a son that any man would be proud to call such, and I hope that he is now the man you are proud to call your husband, that you will cherish and love him for ever.

My dears, I couldn't have wished or hoped for anything more wonderful than the two of you at last finding each other. I hope that you love each other, that you will have a family together, and that you will grow old together. Do so with all my love.

Be assured that I am now with my Heather, and that

the two of us will always be with you, too. Our pride and love for you both will never change.

James.

'Dear God…!' Rufus groaned emotionally, tears in his own eyes as he turned to look at Gabriella.

'Oh, James…!' Gabriella choked, the tears running unchecked down her cheeks.

Rufus reached out to gather her in his arms. 'You are the love of my heart, of my life, and I swear to you I will never let anyone or anything ever harm you again!' he vowed fiercely.

'And you're the love of my life, too, the man I'm proud to call my husband, and I will cherish and love you all my life,' Gabriella assured him as she clung to him.

Their son, James Heath Gresham, born three months later, was a very welcome addition to their already loving family.

Men who can't be tamed...or so they think!

Meet the guy who breaks the rules to get exactly
what he wants, because he is...

HARD-EDGED & HANDSOME

He's the man who's impossible to resist.

RICH & RAKISH

He's got everything—and needs nobody...
until he meets one woman.

He's RUTHLESS!

In his pursuit of passion; in his world the winner takes all!

Billionaire Sebastian Armstrong thinks he knows his
housekeeper inside out. But beneath Emily's plain-Jane
workday exterior there's a passionate woman trying to
forget she's fallen in love with her handsome boss.

THE RUTHLESS
MARRIAGE PROPOSAL
by Miranda Lee

On sale June 2007.

REQUEST YOUR FREE BOOKS!

HARLEQUIN *Presents* ®

2 FREE NOVELS PLUS 2 FREE GIFTS!

PASSION
GUARANTEED
SEDUCTION

YES! Please send me 2 FREE Harlequin Presents® novels and my 2 FREE gifts. After receiving them, if I don't wish to receive any more books, I can return the shipping statement marked "cancel." If I don't cancel, I will receive 6 brand-new novels every month and be billed just $3.80 per book in the U.S., or $4.47 per book in Canada, plus 25¢ shipping and handling per book and applicable taxes, if any*. That's a savings of close to 15% off the cover price! I understand that accepting the 2 free books and gifts places me under no obligation to buy anything. I can always return a shipment and cancel at any time. Even if I never buy another book from Harlequin, the two free books and gifts are mine to keep forever.

106 HDN EEXK 306 HDN EEXV

Name	(PLEASE PRINT)	
Address		Apt. #
City	State/Prov.	Zip/Postal Code

Signature (if under 18, a parent or guardian must sign)

Mail to the **Harlequin Reader Service**®:
IN U.S.A.: P.O. Box 1867, Buffalo, NY 14240-1867
IN CANADA: P.O. Box 609, Fort Erie, Ontario L2A 5X3

Not valid to current Harlequin Presents subscribers.

Want to try two free books from another line?
Call 1-800-873-8635 or visit www.morefreebooks.com.

* Terms and prices subject to change without notice. NY residents add applicable sales tax. Canadian residents will be charged applicable provincial taxes and GST. This offer is limited to one order per household. All orders subject to approval. Credit or debit balances in a customer's account(s) may be offset by any other outstanding balance owed by or to the customer. Please allow 4 to 6 weeks for delivery.

Your Privacy: Harlequin is committed to protecting your privacy. Our Privacy Policy is available online at www.eHarlequin.com or upon request from the Reader Service. From time to time we make our lists of customers available to reputable firms who may have a product or service of interest to you. If you would prefer we not share your name and address, please check here. ☐

HP07

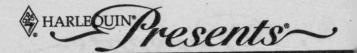